THE EYRIE

By the time this issue reaches the stand, *Weird Tales* will have entered its sixtieth year, so this is by way of being an anniversary issue to The Unique Magazine. By this issue, the 287th, we have published (at a conservative estimate), some 14,713,000 words . . . yes, fourteen *million*, seven hundred and thirteen thousand words of the finest stories in the modern literature of the macabre.

As seems only befitting, we are celebrating this anniversary in a "unique" manner: that is, we are happy to present herein two contributions, written especially for *Weird Tales*, by two writers who, between them, represent virtually the entire history of this extraordinary magazine. The first of these is Frank Belknap Long, who made his first appearance in these pages in 1924, our second year of publication. Mr. Long, a youthful protegé of the great H.P. Lovecraft and a prolific and gifted writer in his own right, has contributed fiction and verse to no fewer than

(continued on page 286)

MORE FANTASTIC READING!

THE WARLORD   (1189, $3.50)
by Jason Frost
California has been isolated by a series of natural disasters. Now, only one man is fit to lead the people. Raised among Indians and trained by the Marines, Erik Ravensmith is a deadly adversary—and a hero of our times!

ORON #5: THE GHOST ARMY   (1211, $2.75)
When a crazed tyrant and his army comes upon a village to sate their lusts, Oron stands between the warmonger and satisfaction—and only a finely-honed blade stands between Oron and death!

ORON   (994, $1.95)
Oron, the intrepid warrior, joins forces with Amrik, the Bull Man, to conquer and rule the world. Science fantasy at its best!

THE SORCERER'S SHADOW   (1025, $2.50)
In a science fantasy of swords, sorcery and magic, Akram battles an ageless curse. He must slay Attluma's immortal sorceress before he is destroyed by her love.

ORON: THE VALLEY OF OGRUM   (1058, $2.50)
When songs of praise for Oron reach King Ogrum's ears, Ogrum summons a power of sorcery so fearsome that Oron's mighty broadsword may melt into a useless lump of steel!

Available wherever paperbacks are sold, or order direct from the Publisher. Send cover price plus 50¢ per copy for mailing and handling to Zebra Books, 475 Park Avenue South, New York, N.Y. 10016. DO NOT SEND CASH.

Weird Tales #4

Edited by Lin Carter

ZEBRA BOOKS
KENSINGTON PUBLISHING CORP.

ZEBRA BOOKS

are published by

KENSINGTON PUBLISHING CORP.
475 Park Avenue South
New York, N.Y. 10016

Printed in the United States of America

Summer, 1983   Vol. 48, No. 4

LIN CARTER, EDITOR
Associates: Roy Torgeson, Robert Weinberg

The Next Glade
By Robert Aickman

It was only a few steps, but it was a world away . . .

The Next Glade

by Robert Aickman

The man looked into her eyes quite steadily, but he certainly didn't smile. "I am coming to see you tomorrow. Tomorrow afternoon," he said.

Noelle didn't smile either. "You don't even know where I live."

"I know very well," he said. Obviously, it would have been easy enough for him to have found out from Simon and Mut, the hosts of the party, but it seemed strange that he should have done so before even meeting Noelle, before ever setting eyes upon her, and almost certainly before being told anything about her. Not until that moment had he implied that he already knew anything at all about her. But it would have been absurd for Noelle to ask how he knew where she lived.

"I'll call for you about three tomorrow. We'll go for

a walk in the woods." There were woods in almost every direction where Noelle lived, but that was true of much of this part of Surrey. She thought about the wood across the road from her gate.

"I don't promise to be there," she said.

"Then I shall have to take a chance that you will be," the man replied. "We mustn't leave it like this, and we'll get no further now."

"What's your name, anyway?" she asked. At that moment Mut turned up the volume on the record-player, and further speech became difficult. Simon and Mut conducted their parties like dress-rehearsals for a play; as little as possible was left to chance.

The man, without smiling, receded into the din. Noelle wondered if he were making a date with another woman, or if he were going home. For him, the party might already have fulfilled its promise . . .

Only when her husband, Melvin, was on his travels, did Noelle go to these parties where almost everyone was younger than she. But that was quite frequently, so she realized how lucky she was that people like Simon and Mut still could be bothered with her.

As it happened, a surprising number of men seemed still to fall fractionally in love with Noelle, and to prefer dulcet and tender talk with her to such other things as might be on offer elsewhere. Noelle could never decide whether it was merely her appearance or something less primary that drew them. She often reflected upon how little she had to complain of.

* * *

Noelle had been perfectly truthful in saying that she couldn't promise. Melvin did sometimes return before this time. As far as she could tell, there was nothing suspicious or ulterior about this. It seemed natural that Melvin should be blown hither and tither by the trade wind, because everyone else was. Gone are the days of predictable grind in the high-stooled counting houses; settled for a lifetime. Business has changed completely, as businessmen always point out.

Besides, Judith or Agnew might be sent home from school early. That sometimes occurred. And if she was in the house when one or the other of them arrived, she had to give much time either to listening to a tale of grievance, or to anxious effort in trying to discover what could have happened this time.

But, when the moment came, the clock struck three, and the doorbell was ringing.

The man was politely extending his hand. "My name is John Morley-Wingfield. With a hyphen, I fear. Let's get that over to start with."

His expression was serious, but not sad. His brown hair curled pleasantly, but not unduly, and was at perhaps its most impressive moment, fading in places, but not yet too seriously grey. His brown eyes were sympathetic without being sentimental. His grab was relaxed with being perfunctory.

For Noelle, hesitation would have served no purpose. "Do come in for a little," she said. "My children return from school in an hour."

"Are they doing well?"

"Not very. If you'll sit down, I'll bring us a cup of tea."

"We must keep enough time for our walk."

She looked at him. "The wood's not all that big. None of them are round here."

He sat on the leathery, cushiony settee, and gazed

11

at his brightly polished brown shoes. "I always think a wood is much the same, however big or small it is. Within reason, of course. The impact is the same. At least upon me."

"You don't actually get lost in these particular woods," said Noelle. "You can't."

He glanced up at her. It was plain that he took all this for delay, wanted them to make a start.

"I'll hurry with the tea," said Noelle. "Will you be all right? Perhaps you'd care to look at this?"

She gave him the latest "Statist." She did not remark that it was her husband who subscribed to it. The man, who had known her address, probably knew about her husband also.

"Or this might be more cheerful."

She held out a back number of the "National Geographical Magazine." It was Melvin too who subscribed to that, though he complained that he never had time to read it, so that the numbers always lay about unsorted until Noelle gave the children an armful for use as reinforcement in and around the sandpit.

When she came back with the tray, the man was on his feet again, and looking at the books. They were, yet again, Melvin's books. Noelle's were upstairs, not all of them even unpacked, owing to shelf shortage.

"Milk and sugar?"

"A very little milk, please. No sugar."

"I know we *shouldn't,*" said Noelle.

He stooped over so that she could hand him his cup. He had a faint but striking aroma, the smell of a pretty good club.

"Careful," said Noelle.

He drifted, sipping, round the room, as if it had been full of people, or perhaps trees, and every settling place occupied, or, alternatively, gnarled and jagged.

He spoke. "You have the most wonderful hair."

Noelle sat up a little, but said nothing.

"And eyes."

Noelle could not prevent herself dimpling almost perceptibly.

"And figure. It would not be possible to imagine a shape more beautiful."

One trouble was that Noelle simply did not know how true or untrue any of these statements were. She had always found it impossible to make up her mind. More precisely, she sometimes felt one thing, and sometimes almost the complete opposite. One had, if one could, to strike an average among the views expressed or implied by others; and others seemed to spend so much of their time dissumulating.

"Have a chocolate finger?" she said, extending the plate towards him at the full length of her arm. She was wearing a dress with delicate, short sleeves. After all, it was August. Melvin particularly hated August in Pittsburgh, where now he was supposed to be.

"Nothing to eat, thank you."

The man was ranging between the Astronaut's Globe and the pile of skiing journals.

"I like your dress."

"It's very simple."

"You have wonderful taste."

"Stop being so civil, please."

"You seem to me quite perfect."

"Well, I'm not." But she made no further

13

references to any specific defect.

"Have some more tea? Bring me your cup."

"Then we must go," he said. "We really must. I want to see you in your proper element."

She handed up the refilled cup without looking at him. "You're right about one thing," she said. "I do love woods. I only wish they were larger."

"You love all music too," said the man, standing over her.

"Yes."

"And the last moments before sunset in the country-side?"

"Yes."

"And being alone in a quiet spot at noon?"

"I usually have the children's meal to prepare."

"And wearing real silk next to your skin?"

"I am not sure that I ever have."

He dashed the cup back on the tray quite sharply. Noelle could see that it was far from empty.

"Let's go. Let's go now."

She walked out with him just as she was. He followed her down the concrete path. The reason why the gate groaned was that the children like the noise. They swung backwards and forwards on it for hours, and threw fits at the idea of the hinges being oiled.

She crossed the road with the man, surprised that there was no traffic. All life had eased off for a moment. They ascended the worn, earth slope into the wood.

"You be guide," he said.

"I keep telling you it's not the New Forest."

"It's far more attractive."

As it happened, Noelle almost agreed with that; or

at least knew what he might have meant. Melvin and she took the children to the New Forest each year, camping at one of the official sites; and each year she found the New Forest a disappointment.

"You fill the wood with wonder," he said.

"We just go straight ahead, you know," said Noelle. "Really there's not much else. All the other paths come to nothing. They're simply beaten down by the kids."

"And by the wild things," said the man.

"I don't think so."

They were walking side by side now, among the silver birches, and it was true that the voice of the world was becoming much drowsier, the voice of nature more express. It was a Tuesday: probably the best day for such an enterprise.

"Will you permit me to put my arm round your waist?" asked the man.

"I suppose so," said Noelle.

He did it, perfectly; neither limply, nor with adolescent tenacity. Noelle began to fall into sympathetic dissolution. She had a clear thirty-five minutes before her.

"The beeches begin here," she said. "Some of them are supposed to be very old. Nothing will grow around their roots."

"That clears the way for us," said the man.

Hitherto, the path had gone gently upwards, but now it had reached the small ridge and begun to descend. Noelle knew that here the wood widened out. None the less, the broad and beaten track led nowhere, because at the far end of the wood lay private property, heavily farmed. Noelle, if asked, would have been very unsure who owned the wood. It seemed to exist in its own right.

"Glorious trees," said the man. "And you are the spirit of them." He was looking up into the high and heavy branches. His grasp of Noelle was growing neither tighter nor looser: admirable. They walked slowly on.

"That's the end," said Noelle, pointing ahead with her free arm.

Two or three hundred yards before them, the wood ended in a moderate-sized dell or clearing; probably no more than the work of all the people who at this point had rotated and gone back on their tracks, returned up the slope.

"I keep telling you how small the wood is," said Noelle. "Not much bigger than a tent."

"Never mind," said the man, gently. "It doesn't matter. Nothing like that matters."

All the way there had, of course, been strewn rubbish, but at the terminal clearing there was considerable more of it.

"How disgusting!" said Noelle. "What a degredation!"

"Don't look at it," said the man, as before. "Look upwards. Look at the trees. Let's sit down for a moment."

It could not be said that the sections of beech trunk lying about had been hollowed out by the authorities into picnic couches, but the said sections had undoubtedly been sliced and trimmed for public use, and arranged like scatter cushions in a television room. It must have taken weeks to do it, but Noelle was of course accustomed to the scene, and had long ago resolved not to let it upset her. She realized that the vast population of the world had everywhere to be accommodated.

Seated, the man began to cuddle her, and she to sink into it for the time available to her. They were sitting with their backs to the wood end and the farmland beyond. But, after a few moments—precious moments, perhaps—he unexpectedly took away his arm and rose to his feet.

"Forgive me," he said. "I should like to explore for a little. You wait here. I'll soon be back."

"How far are you going?"

"Just into the next glade."

"I must go back in six minutes at the very most now." The constant care of children makes for exactitude in situations of that kind.

Had had taken several steps away before she had finished speaking. Now he stopped and half-turned back towards her. He gazed at her for a perceptible period of time, then turned again, and resumed his course without speaking. Noelle had later to admit to herself that she had been aware at once of some difference between the man's deportment and the deportment of men in general. It was almost as if the man slid or glided, so tutored was his gait.

The man strode elegantly and effectively off into the woodland to her right. Here there was fairly dense brush and scrub, so that the man disappeared quite rapidly. Noelle could hear his brown shoes crushing the twigs and mast. Presumably he was shoving through brushwood, but he seemed to advance very steadily, and soon there was no further sound from him.

Noelle gave him four uneasy minutes, then rose in her turn. She called out: "I shall have to be going. I must go."

There was no response. There was no sign or sound of him.

"Where are you?"

Not even a woodpecker signalled.

Noelle called out much more loudly. "John! John, I have to go."

That was the limit of possible action. She could not be expected to shout for the rest of the afternoon, to mount a one-woman search party. There could be no possible question of the man being lost, as she herself had already remarked.

So there was only one thing for her to do. She walked quickly home, much confused in mind and feeling.

When she had arrived, only a single aspiration was definable: that the man, having emerged from the wood in one way or another, would not reappear at her home when the children were having their tea.

He did not reappear. But Noelle remained in a state of jitters until she retired to her single bed.

The next morning she telephoned Mut. She had not cared to do so while the children were in the house.

"That man at your party. John Morley-Wingfield. Tell me about him."

"John Morley was a nineteenth century politico, darling. He wrote the life of Gladstone. It's a good book in its own way."

"I'm sure it is. But it's a different man."

"It always is a different man, darling."

"I'm speaking of John Morley-Wingfield who was at

18

your party."

"Never heard of him, darling. I don't know half the people by name. Do you want me to ask Simon when he gets back?"

"I think I do. Something rather funny has happened. I'll tell you when I see you."

"What's he look like?"

"Suave and competent. Like a diplomat."

"At *our* party?"

"I got on rather well with him."

"The trouble with you is you don't know your own strength. Never mind. I've written down the name. I'll ask Simon. But don't expect much joy. Any news of Melvin?"

In the event, there was no joy at all, because for some time nothing more was heard from Mut on the subject, and Noelle swiftly passed beyond the stage of wanting to know. She realized that one is often half-picked up by men who soon think better of the idea.

Nothing in the least unusual had happened.

Indeed, the only discernible upshot was that Noelle ceased to walk in the woods: not only in the particular wood opposite her front gate, but all the other woods in the district. Some of them in any case were mere struggling strips of scrubland and thornbush: hardly worth visiting unless one was utterly desperate.

But, one Sunday, four or five months later, Melvin suggested that they go for a stroll with the children. It was because one car had been lent to a business friend, whose own had apparently been stolen; and Noelle had forgotten to license the other. Melvin had been very forgiving, as he always was, always.

"Just give me a minute or two to get kitted out,"

said Melvin.

Noelle knew what that meant, and herself changed into trousers and a lumber jacket. The least she could do was co-operate in those supposedly secondary matters that so often proved to be primary. The children were dressed as pioneers already.

Melvin, when he reappeared, eclipsed them all, as was natural. A casual looker-on could hardly have distinguished him from Wild Bill Hickok, especially as Melvin purchased most of his fun gear in the States.

There could be no question of going anywhere but into the wood, because for anything else a motor would have been needed. The children were permitted to walk to and from school, because Noelle had put her foot down and refused to tie herself to driving them so short a distance four times a day. Melvin in turn put his foot down when the possibility arose of the mites straggling along the highway at any other time.

"Don't forget it may rain," said Melvin.

Of course, Noelle had felt certain qualms from the outset, and as soon as they were among the silver birches, she rejoiced that at least she was so differently arrayed, all but in disguise. Moreover, the woods always felt quite different when one entered them with one's entire family. The things that happened when one was with one's family were amazingly unlike the things that happened when one was not. It was this fact that made the transition between the one state and the other always so upsetting.

"Just wait till we meet a buffalo," said Melvin to the children.

Agnew screamed with delight, but Judith hitched at

her belt and looked cynical.

"Got your lasso ready, son?" asked Melvin.

Agnew twirled it round his head and started leaping about among the tangled tree roots. Judith also began to run about, holding her arms in front of her above her head, and bringing them together at short intervals, as if she were catching butterflies, which she was not. There were no butterflies. There never were many.

"I am dead to the world," said Melvin softly to Noelle, when the two children were at what could be regarded as a safe distance, short though that distance really was. "I'm fagged out." In the home circle, Melvin expressed himself conservatively, domestically. He never used the words he used at work.

"You look a bit pale," said Noelle, without turning to him. She had noticed it ever since his return home the day before yesterday. Pallor of any kind would be quite incompatible with his ranch-hand rig.

"I don't know what I'm going to do, Noelle," he went on. "My head feels as if it will burst. I've felt sicker and sicker ever since that February bust-up in Edmonton."

To Noelle it seemed that Melvin went to Edmonton more often than to anywhere else, and that always it lead to trouble, though that last time had doubtless been the worst of all, because Melvin had spoken of it ever since, shaking with rage and bafflement. Edmonton in Alberta, of course; not John Gilpin's homely Edmonton.

"You'd better lay up," said Noelle. "I expect we can afford it."

"No such thing," said Melvin, with what Noelle

deemed an unreasonable darkness in his tone. He had never permitted Noelle to look for a part-time job. It was one of those things about which she was never sure whether she was glad or sorry. She knew that she lacked any specific qualifications.

"I can't let up for a single day," said Melvin. "I'd be shot out if I did. Make no mistake about that."

She supposed that there he must be right. Many of her acquaintances had husbands who had been declared redundant, as the usage now was.

The matter was settled for the moment by Agnew falling over, his feet and legs entangled in his lariat, as if he'd been a steer.

Noelle hoicked him up. She had the readiness of experience, as with an acrobat or exhibition wrestler.

"No bones broken," she said, stroking Agnew's stylishly unbarbered locks. "No blood spilt. No nasty bruise." One could not really know about the last, but it was the thing one said, and very possibly the utterance terminated the danger.

Judith was still running about catching phantom moths. She was a lissom, leggy little girl, but already deep, much as Noelle herself was deep.

"You was riding the range," said Melvin, stubbing Agnew between the shoulders with mock manliness. "You've had a spill, but you're up again, and riding high."

"It was the silly rope," said Agnew.

"Ride on, cowboy," directed Melvin.

"Why should he?" enquired Judith at some distance and to no-one in particular, no-one short of the universe.

"Get going," called out Melvin. "Show 'em. Prove it."

Agnew looked doubtful, but began once more to plunge about. Fortunately, they had now reached the beeches, where the roots, though thicker, were for that reason more noticable. Agnew had begun to use his lasso as if it were a fishing line. All the pockets in the roots were full of fish. Some of them actually did contain a little water. It had been raining on and off for many weeks. Noelle had been going everywhere in a stylish mackintosh.

"I'm nearing the end of the line," said Melvin to Noelle. "Something will just have to give, or I shall break."

The children began running down the slope to the cleared space at the end, where everyone turned and went back up again. The relatively long-limbed Judith, unencumbered with miniature ranch-gear, arrived first. She started an Ashanti dance she had seen on television at school.

Noelle's heart began to beat faster with every descending step. She had forgotten how all courage leaves one when the peril, whatever it be, is really close in time or space.

"I've thought of applying for a transfer," said Melvin. "I haven't told you, because I didn't want to worry you." He was trying to struggle out of his trapper's jerkin, though the weather was no warmer than it had been, and Noelle felt chillier every minute.

They were all assembled in the clearing. The litter was now sodden, much of it eaten away by rats. There was no other human being visible, or even audible.

"Well, there's nothing else to do but go back," said Noelle almost immediately.

"No!!!" At school the children had learned the trick of negating loudly in unison.

"Let's sit down for a moment," said Melvin.

"It's all too soggy," protested Noelle.

"I've got 'The Frontiersman' from last time," proclaimed Melvin, producing it from the rustler's pocket in his cast-off jerkin. "I'll rip it up and we can take half each. I never have time to read it anyway."

"We can't sit among so much litter. It's disgusting. It's degrading."

But Melvin was settled on one of the tree trunks and was chivalrously holding out the bigger portion of the bisected journal.

"Just for a moment, Noelle," he said wistfully, all but smiling at her. "I need to get back some part of my sanity."

So she slumped on the trunk beside him. She tried hard to keep her bottom on the small, thin package. "Don't go too far away," she said to the children. "We're only stopping here for a minute."

Melvin had drawn his lumberjack's knife, and was running his finger along the blade. His gaze was at once concentrated and absent-minded. Fortunately, the blade was unlikely to be very sharp.

"I often dream of what it *should* have been like," said Melvin. "On some island. Our island. You in a grass skirt, me in a leopardskin, sun all the time, and breadfruit, and mangoes, and coconuts, and flying fish. All day and all night the throbbing of the surf on the reef, and every now and then a distant schooner to wave to. Birds of paradise sweeping from palm tree to palm tree. Monkeys chattering and swinging. Loving you on the warm sand in the darkness beneath the

Southern Cross."

"Beautiful," said Noelle, gently taking his hand. "I'd like that." Melvin looked at her doubtfully. Agnew often had just that same look, inherited or acquired.

"I mean it. Truly," said Noelle softly. "I'd like it too. But we have to be practical." She could not help squirming a little on the tiny, extemporised cushion.

"Do we? Must we?" He was drawing the lumber knife across the back of his hand.

"Of course we must, darling. I'm sure we can work something out together. Something practical."

She always said that, and she would have been sincerely pleased if it had ever proved possible. What happened every time in actuality was that she had nearly expired of combined boredom and nausea before Melvin had made any real progress in describing the full details of the particular crisis. She never doubted that Melvin's business life was truly terrible. One trouble was that a terrible life is less fulfilling to others than a happy life.

He squeezed her hand. "If the men in white coats don't come for me first," he said.

"I'll keep them away," she smiled. "I'll distract their attention."

Inevitably, the children, forbidden to go far, were enjoying themselves among the litter. They were investigating discarded food and drink cans, deciphering sodden letterpress, speculating about indelicate proprietary utilities. Really they were only a few feet away. All along, surreptitiousness had been enforced upon the parental intimacies.

"You'd distract anyone's attention, Noelle," said

25

Melvin, almost whispering.

Noelle looked away from his fatigued face and glanced for a moment towards the thicker foliage to the right of the clearing.

"I'd like you to distract mine this very moment," said Melvin, sotto voce.

"We must be *practical*," said Noelle.

Melvin threw the knife into the ground, though it failed to enter, and merely lay horizontally, adding to the litter.

"Children!" he called out. "Run away and play for a bit."

Noelle rose. "No, don't," she called to them.

Confused, the children came to a standstill before reaching the thicket towards which they had started charging. They began playing triangles on the rough ground. It was a game that everyone was playing and involved much darting about in a small area. Preferably, there should have been more players, but Agnew and Judith were still young enough to improvise.

"We can't possibly," said Noelle to Melvin. "We'll stay just a few more minutes, so the children can have a run about, and I'll see if I can get them to bed a little earlier than usual."

"I want you *now*," said Melvin.

Noelle smiled at him, but said nothing.

"*Now*," said Melvin. He picked up the knife and reattached it to its thong. "Let's get lost in the forest. The kids won't even notice for a long time."

Melvin often had whims of that kind. Noelle supposed them to be outlets for the pressure under which so much of his life was passed.

He rose to his feet and pulled Noelle to hers. "Let's see how lost we can get."

She had found it best at such moments to go along with him as far as was practicable. At the moment, it was quite true that the children seemed absorbed in their running and tumbling. Triangles is a far more physically demanding game than ring-a-ring-a-roses. The children seemed not even to notice their parents departing across the clearing; exactly as Melvin had said. And, after all, there was no real reason why Noelle should not enter those bushes.

"I don't think we shall get *lost*," she said. "It's just into the next glade."

"Have you been there?"

"Not really."

"Then how do you know? When we stray from the warpath, we enter the impenetrable rain forest."

All the same, Noelle did know. She had a mental picture of what it was like on the other side of the bushes. She always had had. She must have been there some time, though she could not remember the circumstances.

"It's impossible to get lost in these woods," she said. "Or in any of the other woods round here."

Melvin had produced the knife once more, with a view to hacking and slashing a path for them.

"Truly, it's not as dense as that," said Noelle. "A very little pushing will do it. You could almost get through in evening dress."

So, though the whole idea was Melvin's, it was she who went ahead, while he made a more proper job of it.

Duly, she was through the thicket in about ninety

seconds, and in the next glade. As she expected, it was quiet there, reassuring; unlittered, because untracked. The trees were taller and more dignified. There was an element of natural architecture, an element of mystery. Foliage hid the sky, moss the ground.

The moss was so deep and so apparently virgin as, in the exact present circumstances, to be suggestive. Noelle paddled through it across the width of the glade. The children might be temporarily out of touch with their parents, and she was fleetingly out of touch with Melvin, left farther behind than mere yards would account for. She could not even hear his wood-manship exercises; perhaps because she was not particularly listening for them.

She entered the trees on the far side of the glade; not in the least overwhelming, all conforming to perfectly acceptable proportions. Beyond this, however, she was sure she had never penetrated; and she was very aware of it. She had no idea of what she might find, though she knew perfectly well how small was the scope.

She stopped. She had reached the end of the world already; even sooner than she had expected. It was marked by a tangle of wire: several different varieties and brands of wire; stretching between rotten, leaning posts, with woodlice at their feet.

There was a house, timbered but not thatched. The large windows were filled with diamond panes. There was a squinting figure in artificial stone above the garden door. Much of the detail was monastic in style. There was a very neat hedge all round the rectangular garden, every item in which was perfect. The hedge was low enough for Noelle to see across it where it ran parallel with the tangled boundary.

A man was digging a hole in one of the garden beds. For the purpose, a quantity of blooms had been displaced. Indeed, one might well define the new artifact not as a hole but as a trench. The man was in his braces and wore a shirt and tie, as if he were acting upon impulse. They seemed to be an elegant, silk shirt, and a handsome moire tie. His was the only figure in sight, except for a mammal of some kind which scuffled up and down in a small cage near the house. The man was concentrating on his work, and a minute or two passed before there was any question of his looking up.

As far as Noelle was concerned, it was unnecessary for him to look up. She knew quite well who he was. If the wires in front of her had been taut instead of tangled, she would have clutched at and clung to them.

It had at no time occurred to her that John Wingfield-Morley was a neighbour. At least it explained whither he had so casually disappeared. Furthermore, if he possessed a house of the type before her, he almost certainly possessed a wife and family also. Everything seemed unbelievably normal and familiar. There was even the pet in its cage.

But still she could not move or look away. This was to be turned into a pillar of salt, even if only provisionally, and even though Melvin must surely be coming up behind her, with a knife in one hand, a miniature axe in the other. Necessarily, the man before her, almost certainly unaccustomed to steady manual effort, would soon be taking a short breather.

In an instant, he looked straight into Noelle's eyes.

Though his hair was hardly disarranged, his face was a confused mask, surrounding eyes filled with horror, eyes so large as to suggest that they would never again be their former size.

Noelle turned and ran. She managed, as everyone does at such times, to avoid all the roots and briars. Within seconds, she was tripping back across the tranquil, unvisited glade. Within a minute, she was making a disturbance. She was calling "Melvin! Melvin!"

Melvin answered. "Here, curse it."

Before she could find him, she was out on the other side of the thicket. The children had at that very moment stopped playing, and were strolling towards her.

"What's the matter, mummy? Has something happened?"

"I'm *here*," roared out Melvin, from among the bushes. "Blast it."

"I think your father may have hurt himself," said Noelle. "Let's go see if we can help, shall we?"

Melvin's left hand was streaming with blood. "We must get you home as soon as possible and tie you up. You must lie down and rest, and Agnew and Judith will go to bed as quietly as mice."

"*Why* must we?" asked Judith.

But Agnew was good and helpful all the way back.

This time Noelle remained in a state of jitters for considerably longer than on the previous occasion; and her nerviness was exacerbated by the unexpected complications that followed Melvin's mishap. He was required to remain at home and in bed, while his

Week followed week, and as it became more and more necessary to be sensible, it became more and more difficult. Noelle suspected that the doctors were baffled, though they never said so. Certainly she herself had begun to find life as a whole baffling as never before. It was all but impossible to decide how big a step it was appropriate to take.

Judith had begun to ail in various different ways, two or three of them at a time; fundamentally the trouble lay in her anxieties about her Daddy, and her doubts about her Mummy. Agnew, on the other hand, had quieted down and become a quite nice little boy. It was as when a running bull calf ceases to be chivvied and goaded. Noelle began in small ways to confide in him; in trifles, positively to rely upon him.

One night the telephone rang. It was well after eleven. "Get up please, darling," said Noelle to Agnew, whose unkempt head lay in her lap. "Just for a second." Agnew responded quite obligingly.

"Hello. Oh it's you, Mut."

"Come to a party on Friday. Sorry to be so late in asking you. It'll be the usual people and the usual things."

"I don't think I'd better, Mut."

"It'll take you out of yourself."

"No, not really."

Agnew was gazing at her with big eyes, though less big than those other eyes, which she saw so much of the time.

"Thank you very much, none the less," said Noelle. "It's sweet of you."

"How *is* Melvin, anyway?"

"Worse, as far as I can tell. The doctors seem to be baffled."

"Seriously, Noelle, I suggest the time has come to fetch him home. Where he is, it's the blind leading the blind."

Agnew had crept up to her on the floor, and was nuzzling into her thigh.

"I daresay you're right, Mut. But you know how bad I am as a nurse. You'll remember for yourself how hopeless I always was."

"I remember," said Mut. "In that case, I suggest you come to the party. At least, it will take your mind off."

"I'm not sure it will. It didn't the last time."

"You mean the mystery man. Simon's got a new idea about *him*. From your description, he thinks he can only have been a man called John Martingale, who lives quite near you. He's supposed to have a lovely garden."

"I don't want to talk about it," said Noelle. "There's been far too much from it. I'll try to tell you one day."

"I'm sure the whole thing's a phantasy, as I said before."

"It is, and yet it isn't," said Noelle.

"Oh, it's like that!" said Mut. "Then come to our party and take your mind off *two* things. I think you need a change."

"Thank you, Mut, but no. Really no. Please ask me next time."

"Well, of course I shall. The best possible about Melvin. And from Simon."

The impression made upon Noelle, as she put back the receiver, was that Agnew had drawn himself tightly together in the manner of a small soapstone idol. He was squatting there like a holy pussycat.

Never once in years had she noticed anything so peculiar about him, not even when he had been a baby.

"Well, darling?" she said to him, a little cautiously.

He looked at her, and then crawled back to her. She caught him up, set him on her knee, and hugged him.

Almost at once, the telephone rang again. Noelle clung on to Agnew, and managed to stretch out her arm, supposing it to be renewed supplication from her best friend, Mut.

"Yes, it's me," she said, and giving Agnew a squeeze.

But it wasn't Mut.

"Is that Mrs. Corcoran?"

"It is."

"Mrs. Melvin Corcoran?"

"Yes."

"Then you'll remember me at the hospital. I'm sorry to say I have some bad news."

There was a woman who lived half a mile away named Kay Steiner. When Noelle had gone to parties in Melvin's absence, Kay Steiner had almost always taken the children for the night. They seemed to like going to her. They managed, both of them, to praise the food and they both appeared to respond to her way with them. Mrs. Steiner had no children of her own, but she was not a widow. It was merely that her husband, Franklin, was often away from home for long periods. Noelle fancied she had never been told what he did at these times, or at any other time, but he seemed nice enough in his own way. About Kay

Steiner there could be no doubt of any kind. Kay was a brick.

After the funeral, Noelle had a quiet talk with the solicitor, who remarked that it might be useful if the position of things were roughly indicated by him as soon as possible.

He asked if their talk could be attended also by Mr. Mullings, who was an executor. Noelle had several times entertained Melvin's friend, Ted Mullings, to dinner or supper, and she knew that the other executor, who was rather elderly, had been indicated simply for form. Ted Mullings had already played a prominent part at the funeral, to which he had driven all the way in his Jaguar from his home near Sandgate, having taken a day off from business for the purpose.

At the end of the discussion, which was short, the future stretching before Noelle and the children seemed as open as it could possibly be. She would have to create an entirely new world for them. Noelle looked white. What Americans call challenge never brought out the best in her.

They had all had tea after the funeral itself, but, during the talk with the legal people, Kay Steiner had been quietly preparing a small second one, for consumption before the men went their ways.

Trying to lap down her fifth or sixth cup, Noelle reflected that in three weeks she would be thirty-eight. Kay Steiner did not know this, though of course Mut did, who would never tell. The children knew the date, and celebrated it, naturally, but had not been told the full facts. Now, perhaps, they need not know for a long time. Noelle also reflected how strange it was to be dressed quite ordinarily for her husband's requiem.

Anyone could see that she was worn out. Kay suggested that she take in Judith and Agnew for a few days, so that Noelle would have time to find her feet. The children were not in the room at the time, and Noelle accepted with hardly a demur. Judith had been weeping excessively, and was now lying down. Agnew had been looking paler and more mature every moment.

There was resistance at the time of departure, but Kay dealt with it skillfully, and Ted Mullings offered a ride to Kay's house in his Jaguar. Agnew stepped in ahead of everyone, but Judith declined furiously to go at all, and had to be dragged all the way by Kay, while Agnew waited on her doorstep.

The solicitor had a quantity of work to take home, especially as he had been away from the office for so much of the day; the thereafter Noelle was alone in the house. She had declined Kay's offer to take her in also for that one night at least. She had thinking to do, and so might help the process, though she was far from sure whether or not they would.

It was autumn and she threw the remains of the funeral baked meal into the fire. Melvin had always insisted upon as many open grates as possible, and today one of them had been put into use. Noelle really had to stand over the daily woman, Clarice, while it was done. She disliked such exercises in authority exceedingly.

The clock struck six. Noelle felt like midnight, but at least there was a reasonable amount of time for all the thinking she would have to do; all the bricks she would have to make without the right kind of experience, or the proper temperament.

She could scarcely make herself another cup of tea; scarcely even want another cup. She picked up a boomerang she had brought from Darwin. The boomerang was not a commercially produced plaything, he had said, but a real weapon. Since, it had lain on his desk. Noelle dandled it wistfully. That was of course packed with all kinds of things that would have to be disposed of somehow; and profitably, if possible. Not even Melvin's life insurance had proved to be of a kind best suited the circumstances as they had turned out. Noelle realized that she must start thinking at once. Her situation was considerably better that in which many widows found themselves. She knew that well.

But the bell rang.

It was not yet ten minutes past six. Doubtless someone had left something behind. Instantly, it occurred to Noelle that she herself had been left behind. She flushed for a second and managed to open the door.

The man from the house on the other side of the wood was standing there. Naturally, he showed no sign of the disarray in which Noelle had last seen him. His eyes were quite unstaring. This time he even wore a hat, though he swept it off as the door opened. He spoke at once.

"I was so sorry to hear of your loss. I did not think it right to intrude upon the funeral, but I should like to do anything I can which might help you. It seems to me the sort of thing that should be said as soon as possible. So here I am to say it, and to say that I really mean it. Perhaps you would permit me to think for you about the many matters that must arise?"

"There are indeed many matters," said Noelle. She felt that she was being watched from the houses on the other side of the road, beyond the worn entrance to the wood.

"Possibly it would help if we ourselves could define our position in the light of the changed circumstances?"

Noelle glanced at him for the first time. "All right," she said. "If you think so. Please come in for a few minutes."

He followed her in. She felt that she should take his hat, but in a modern house there was nowhere in particular to put it.

"I have sent the children away," she said.

He sat on the same sofa; the sofa on which she herself had just been scrying the opaque future.

"This is a boomerang," he said, as if most people would not know.

"It was my husband's."

"Your's is a terrible loss for anyone." Noelle nodded.

"Most of all for a woman as sensitive and highly-strung as you. Your cheeks are wan and your lovely eyes are shadowed."

"I was very fond of my husband."

"Of course. You have a warm heart and a tender soul."

"In some ways he was not very grown-up. I think he needed me."

"Who would not need *you?*"

Noelle hesitated. "Would you care for a glass of sherry?"

"If you will join me."

"Yes, I'll join you. It may be the last sherry I shall see for some time." She filled the two glasses. "I admit that I have been left in a difficult position, Mr. Morley-Wingfield. All this will have to be sold. Everything."

He seemed to smile. "You do not really suppose that I can agree to be addressed by so absurd a name?" He raised his glass. "To the best possible future!" he said very seriously.

"You told me it was your name," said Noelle, not responding to his toast. "Actually, you volunteered the information. What, in fact, *is* your name?"

"My name is John," he said, now undoubtedly smiling, but smiling at her.

"Mut and Simon seem to know nothing about you."

"I can return the compliment. I know little about them. All I know is that I met you in their company. That matters very much. I hope to both of us."

"I think I should tell you," said Noelle, "that I saw you digging in your garden. I was with my husband."

"You are mistaken," he replied. "Never willingly have I held a spade in my hands since I left Harrow."

"Do you know how my husband's illness began?"

"I must acknowledge that I do not."

"We went for a walk in the wood with our children. My husband insisted on breaking through into the next glade, while we left the children playing. He slashed himself quite badly, and he never really got over it. Some kind of blood poisoning, I suppose, but the doctors were baffled. In the end, he died of it."

"It is a sad moment to say such a thing, but I admit to being bad also. I cannot follow the story. It is because you are so upset by everything that's happened, my sweet Noelle."

She thought it was the first time he had addressed her by her name. Indeed, she knew very well that it was.

"That is just what Mut said to me on the telephone. But it's not true. It was when we were in the next glade that we saw you digging and saw you quite clearly."

"So your husband saw me too?"

"No," said Noelle, after a second. "I don't really think he did, he was pre-occupied. But I know perfectly well that *I* did."

"How was I dressed?" asked the man. "Seeing that I was digging then was I got up?" His tone was friendly, perhaps quizzical.

"You had taken off your jacket."

"My dear girl! Whatever next? Was I digging in my braces?"

"As a matter of fact, you were."

The man looked away from her and down at the carpet. He had drained his glass, as had Noelle.

"It all seems rather unlikely," said the man, though only in a tone of mild remonstrance. "The sincerity of your belief," he added, "makes you look more charming and delightful than ever. What suggestions had our mutual friend, Mut, to offer? Another delightful woman, by the way, though a daisy in a spring field, where you are the lovely lily of the world, body and soul and spirit."

He had ceased to fondle the boomerang and was

letting it lie beside him on the cushion. Noelle crossed to the sofa and picked it up. She continued holding on to it.

"Would you like another glass of sherry?"

"If *you* would."

She filled the two glasses and went back to her seat. "Previously," she said, "I had no idea that you lived in the neighborhood. You should have told me."

"But I don't!" he cried. "I merely came to know it from the time I was at Sandhurst. What days those were! The laughing and the grieving!" Then he raised his glass. "I propose another toast. To a bright future erupting from the troubled past!" Again Noelle did not respond.

"We must expect that it will take a little time," he said. "It will be the crown of my life to see the task accomplished."

Noelle almost emptied her glass at a swig.

"You push through into the next glade," she said. "You go straight across it, and beyond the trees and bushes on the far side is a half-timbered house with lots of big windows, and you live there."

"Half-timbered houses do not usually have big windows. I would not live in such a house."

Noelle was twisting the boomerang round and round. There was nothing left of her second glass of sherry.

"What does it matter," cried Noelle, half to herself, hardly at all to the man.

All the same, it did matter: the house was only ten to fifteen minutes away, even when one was walking at the pace of one's children and then struggling through the bushes and undergrowth in a quite sedate manner.

"I came in the hope of helping with any difficulties there might be," said the man, "and plainly this is the first of them. The distance is very short. I suggest we go and look for this house. We both know the way quite well. Besides, the fresh air will do you good."

The mud on the path could not but remind Noelle of the funeral. At the funeral it had drizzled persistently, now it was merely a matter of a penetrating moisture in the air. Noelle was wearing her stylish mackintosh, but the man was unprotected. Noelle feared that his trousers would lose their crease, even that the fine fabric of his suit might lose texture and buoyancy. Already his shoes were streaked and smeared.

"Are you sure you want to go through with this?" she asked him.

"I mean to drive out some of the megrims," he said.

They descended the slope to the clearing. The raininess had left nothing but a mush. One could no longer distinguish plastic bag from squashed balloon; cigarette pack from snapcorn box. Natural forces were mounting a liquidation of their own.

"And now for the next glade!" admonished the man jovially.

"We can't possibly," cried Noelle. "The bushes are soaking. You'll utterly wreck you suit." She made no reference to his hat, which was even more inappropriate.

"We'll be through in an instant," said the man. "If you've done it already, you'll know that."

"It's just your suit," said Noelle. "I know it's not difficult." She mustn't permit him the slightest doubt that she had at least once been through, had seen his house. "You need to dress up for a thing of this kind in such weather." Melvin had always overdone it, as he overdid so many things, but of course he had been basically right.

"I'll take off my hat," said the man, "and then you'll feel better."

They were through in no time. On the other side, Noelle had to admit that she could detect no particular damage to his clothes, apart from his shoes; and that even her own elegantly flowing mackintosh seemed unscathed.

The man had been laughing for a moment, but now the two of them stood silently in the next glade. The trees, the greens and browns, seemed more mysteriously architectural than ever. They too brought back the funeral to her, but she realized that many things would do that, possibly for the rest of her life.

"It has an atmosphere," said Noelle. "I admit that."

"Yes," said the man. "But you are almost the only being who would feel it. You are a wonderful person." she half turned away, then:

The man looked at her.

"I *am* so sorry," said Noelle. "I must be . . . very tired."

"Of course you are tired, sweet Noelle," he said. "You hardly know whether you are on your charming head or your pretty feet." He looked at Noelle's boots. "But we shall change all that. Slowly but surely."

It would have been uncouth of Noelle not to smile, though non-commitally.

"The house you mentioned stands at the other side of the glade?" enquired the man, not too obviously humouring her.

"Through here," said Noelle, pointing.

"More bushes!" cried the man, in mock irony.

"Not such dense ones. Then you come to a barbed-wire fence. All of which you know perfectly well. I'm afraid your shoes will suffer in all this wet moss. But it's entirely your own fault."

"But of course," cried the man. "Please go ahead."

Noelle went on without looking back. She wondered if there were small snakes and horrid insects concealed in the moss which the dampness might bring out.

At the far side, the tapping was distinctly clearer. Noelle looked back. She saw that his shoes were submerged at every pace, that water streamed from them each time he took a step. She knew from experience how wet the bottoms of one's trousers become at such moments.

"Are you all right?" she enquired weakly.

"Go on, go on," the man said. "Go on as though I were not here."

Noelle considered for a moment. "All right," she decided. "I shall."

But through the second belt of trees and bushes, and short though this part of the journey was, she advanced far more slowly.

The truth was that now there was no other sound at all but that of the tapping, the hammering, the clanking—perhaps even clanging. It seemed to Noelle that the din was rising in a degree entirely out of proportion with the distance she was covering.

She realized perfectly well, however, that the noise was nothing to that on a reasonably large modern building site. There was always something for which to be grateful when one made the effort to see life in that way.

Furthermore, all the disfiguring barbed-wire seemed to have vanished or been taken away; at least for as far in either direction that Noelle could see.

The hedge round the garden was still there, low and thin, but now sadly shredded, shrivelled. *The costly-looking, half-timbered house seemed not to be there.* Noelle compelled herself to advance across the line which once the barbed-wire had marked. At that moment, she realized that what was happening to her now was like going "over the top."

She peered downwards over the tattered hedge. There was the enormous hole or cavity; excessively diametered, far deeper than Noelle could discern.

All down the hole men were working. Hundreds of men — thousands, she might have been forgiven for thinking. Sooner rather than later, she realized that women too were working down there: to start with, at typewriters, at comptometers, at computers. Noelle knew these things from the days when she had herself worked in offices.

There was noise enough in all conscience, for any auditor who was fully human; but Noelle soon realized that probably the noise was nothing like enough for everything that was being actually done. The comparison with the modern building site recurred to her. Properly, there should have been far *more* noise. She was sure of it. Perhaps that was the most alarming thought of all.

Noelle turned round and stood with her back squared against the garden hedge. She looked in every direction for the man who had challenged her to this strange experience.

John Morley-Wingfield, like the once-tangled wire, was no longer visible. His apparition was no more finite than his name. Of course, not withstanding his talk, he might have failed at the last thicket; might have decided upon some care, after all, for his suit; might even have retreated before the moss crossing, and be composedly awaiting Noelle on her own side of the glade.

His case would in some degree have been made. Noelle had seen for herself that, in the strictest construction of words, there was no half-timbered house with overlarge windows. Possibly, indeed, Mr. Morley-Wingfield was a property speculator who had demolished his dwelling to set up a factory on the site, or an office-block. Few of Melvin's friends would have seen much to criticise in that.

The moisture in the air had begun to precipitate heavily also to darken the sky. Right through the experience, Noelle had realized, at the back of her mind, how late in the day it was. Possibly the second most alarming thing of all was that at such an hour all these entities were still at work.

One could call this nothing but rain. It was beginning to soak through. She wondered if there was a way out of the wood by turning right up the glade: a short cut. She had no wish ever again in her life, to meet those furbelows of parched or sodden trash at the point where people turned; to behold those deftly shaped official seats.

But turning right up the unknown, moss-bottomed glade would be far too much of a further new experience at this of all moments. The glade might appear indifferent to her, but, even in a suburban wood, the coming of darkness could bring unexpected risks, as poor Melvin had so often emphasized.

Indeed, while reflecting in this way, Noelle had almost recrossed the spongy moss, which this time seemed less likely to harbour leeches and freshwater scorpions than to be in itself vaguely bottomless. Had John Morley-Wingfield simply sunk through a particularly soft spot?

She pushed into the familiar bushes. At this point the noise of the rain had become loud enough to drown the faint thumping and tip-tapping of the over-time workers.

Noelle could not hold back a cry. The briar immediately before her was still splashed with blood; exactly as when she had last seen it. The weeks and months of rain had made no difference at all.

Up the slope from where the rubbish rotted, down the gentler slope through the silver birches, Noelle, encumbered by her boots, ran for home, with half-shut eyes. She was quite surprised to find her home still there.

But she did not enter the house: partly because the man might soon be there too; partly, perhaps mainly, for wider reasons still.

Instead she walked to Kay Steiner's house. Though winded by her up-hill and down-dale run, she walked briskly. But surely it was by now too dark for the neighbours to continue watching her . . .

"I've changed my mind. Can I please stay the night too?"

"Of course you can, dear! I always thought it would

be the best thing. I hated leaving you in that gloomy house."

"Yes, it *was* a gloomy house, wasn't it?"

Kay Steiner looked at Noelle. "Well," she ventured, "in all the circumstances—"

"No. It was not that only."

"Really? In that case you'd better all move in here until Franklin gets back. Now take off your boots and your wet clothes. These smart macs never keep out the rain, do they? I'll lend you some clothes, if you like. Perhaps I ought to tell you that Judith is a little feverish. I think it's because she fought so hard on the way here. She's been refusing anything to eat or drink, and she's been screaming. It's nothing to worry about, of course. I'll lend you a thermometer so that you can take her temperature yourself during the night."

Kay had laid the table beautifully, and with lighted candles; as if it had been a special occasion. She was at work in the kitchen. The many surfaces were strewn with comestibles and accessories. Kay wore an apron; the Cook Book lay open.

"I see no reason why we shouldn't make the best of things," said Kay. "I'm glad you like that sweater. It's my favourite. It was given me in rather romantic circumstances."

They consumed several glasses of sherry and a whole bottle of wine. Franklin Steiner belonged to a wine club connected with a well-known firm, which made the selections: neither costly nor cheap.

"Let's have coffee in the lounge," said Kay ultimately.

* * *

"Tell me," said Noelle, while Kay was filling the cups. "Have you ever taken a lover? Since you married Franklin, I mean."

"Yes," said Kay. "I've taken, as you call it, several."

Kay passed across the cup. All the things belonged to a set which Franklin had bought somewhere upon impulse at an auction.

"Does it make any difference?" asked Noelle.

"To what, dear?"

"To your feelings for Franklin. To the nature of your marriage."

"Most certainly not. How serious you are!"

"Yes," said Noelle. "I think I am serious."

"It takes all sorts," said Kay.

Noelle began to stir her coffee. "Did you ever know a man calling himself John Morley-Wingfield?"

"If you mean was he one of them, the answer is No. Mine didn't have names like that."

"He may be a neighbour," said Noelle. "But you never heard of him?"

"Never," said Kay. "And I don't believe you did either. You've just dreamed him up."

Wearing Kay's nightdress, Noelle lay unsleeping in one of Kay's beds. As Kay had no children, there were no fewer than four spare rooms in the house; and as Kay was Kay, all four were always available. It was just as well at such times as this.

The door opened quietly. In the stream of light from the passage, Noelle could see Agnew's wild head.

"Mummy."

"What is it, darling?"

"Who was that man you were walking with after I

came here? Was it Daddy?"

Certainly the almost total darkness was something of an immediate relief to Noelle.

"Of course it wasn't Daddy, Agnew. It was someone quite different. But how did you see him?"

"Mrs. Steiner was making a fuss about Judith, so I was bored, and just ran home. What man was he, Mummy?"

"He was a friend of Daddy's who couldn't come earlier. There are always people like that in life. You must never let them upset you."

"Mummy, are you going to marry him?"

"I don't think so, Agnew. I'm not proposing to marry anyone for some time yet. No one but you."

"Really not, Mummy? Why did you go for a walk with him if he was only Daddy's friend?"

"He wanted to take me out of myself. It was kind of him. You know it's been a difficult day for me, Agnew."

"Are you *sure* that's all, Mummy?"

"Quite sure, Agnew. Now get into bed with me for a little while, and we'll say no more about it, if you please, not even think about it."

Agnew put his arms round her, squeezing himself tightly against her breasts; and all was at peace until the morrow.

Crocuses
By Charles Sheffield

A quietly chilling little masterpiece . . .

Crocuses

by Charles Sheffield

The blue van came nosing along Prospect Street just after lunch on the hottest day of July. Awnings sat out over the shop windows to shield them from the sun and most of the shopkeepers had retired to the rear of the stores, as far away as possible from the dusty glare of the roadway.

The van, a Winnebago with West Virginia license plates, crept along the store fronts, a few yards at a time, and stopped at last in front of Otis Lombard's real estate office. A man climbed down from the driver's seat and peered in through the office window. After a moment he turned and nodded to the woman in the van. He went inside.

Otis Lombard had been pawing helplessly through a pile of papers. He had been to lunch with the Zoning Inspector, and four bottles of beer had washed away any energy into the noon heat. Lombard was perspiring heavily, an overweight man in an over-tight blue suit. He looked up and sighed as the bells on the door tinkled and the stranger entered.

"Mr. Lombard." The visitor was a little below medium height, round-faced and dark-complexioned. He looked about thirty-five years old. His hair was cut in an unfashionable close crop, an inch of spiky dark growth standing up straight above his forehead. Otis Lombard felt the stare of the dark-brown eyes, intense and alert, bright as two pieces of anthracite. He stood up quickly.

"I'm Otis Lombard. What can I do for you?"

"I'm looking for a place to rent for a year or two." He nodded his head to the Winnebago parked outside. "We'd like somewhere with a good bit of land, with hunting on it, well out of town. I don't want to farm it. I'm looking for something with a house and woods and maybe some streamside bottom land."

"Yes, sir." Lombard waved the man to a seat and sat back at his desk. He had noted the frayed lapel on the corduroy jacket and the scuffed, down-at-heel brown shoes. "I can show you something fits that description, no trouble at all. For a two-year lease, the owner'll want four months deposit on it, first one and last three." He pulled a yellow folder from the tray on the corner of his desk and leafed through it. "How much land, and how much are you willing to pay?"

A shrug. "Fifty acres or more. Couple of hundred a month, if I have to. I don't need but one bedroom, and a couple of rooms to live in. The land's the main thing. I want a private place, and I want to be way off the main roads."

Otis Lombard had been watching very closely. The mention of a four months deposit had produced no reaction at all. He pulled a blue sheet from the folder.

"Got one here might do you nicely. Tantalon Farm. Eighty acres, but only sixty feet of road front. Most people don't like small frontage, but I guess you don't mind. You can have it for one-fifty a month. There's a nice old wood frame house on it—two beds, living-room, kitchen, wash-house, unfinished basement. It's got oil furnace, hot water radiators—best sort of heat you can have, for my money. Basement has its own well, good water—tested last year, all right to drink. Let's see, how many of you?"

"Just two of us and a dog."

"You and Mrs.—er?"

"I'm Peter Daniels."

He sat there, stony-eyed, until Otis Lombard realized that was all the information he would be getting. He coughed.

"All right, Mr. Daniels. Let's see, what else do you want to know? We can go right on over and take a look at the property—couple of others, too, on the way there, but they cost a bit more."

"Tell me about the boundary lines. And how's the hunting?"

"Yessir. Boundary lines are clean. You've got a stream runs by on the north and the west. East side has a chain link fence, six feet high, all the way along it. The road and entry is on the south, but the power company holds most of the frontage. They have their own fence, chain link again. Now then, on the hunting." Lombard peered at the cards in his file for a moment or two, then shrugged. "It's not a question we get asked too often. Maybe best if we go over, let you take a look for yourself. You're interested in the property, though?"

"Could be. Let's go and see it." Peter Daniels stood up. He was not tall, but there was a solid and confident look to the way he moved. In the hot office he ought to have been perspiring, as Lombard was perspiring. There was no sign of sweat on his closeshaven round face. "What did you say this place is called?"

"Tantalon Farm, but it's never been a real farm. There's a couple of acres of truck garden near the house, if you want it. The rest's all natural woods." Lombard picked up his folder and went to the wall of the office, where numerous bunches of keys were hanging from hooks. "One thing you'll like about this place, it's supposed to be nice and cool right through the summer. The old name for it was 'The Meeting Place of the Winds', back when the land was first settled. You always get these cross breezes, down by the stream. It's a good property, and it's cheap."

"Yeah." Daniels smiled without showing his teeth. "You might even think it's a bit too cheap. So why's it empty?"

"Most people want a place they can farm." He hesitated. "There's a little bit of local superstition there, too. The last tenant had an accident with his gun, down by the stream. Before that, though, there was a good reputation—the owner lived there for fifty years, before he went on down to Florida to retire."

"I'm not superstitious. Let's go."

"Be right with you. One other thing, if you do decide to take it."

"Yeah?"

"You're from out of town." Otis Lombard ran his finger around the tight collar of his shirt. "I told you, the owner's down in Florida, and he'll ask me some about your financial background. So I was wondering if you have any, you know, bank references, that we could get out of the way before we leave."

"No bank references." Daniels smiled again, this time showing a mirthless display of discolored teeth. "Don't worry about it. Let's see, we'd have two years at a hundred and fifty a month. Who pays utilities?"

"You do."

"All right. That would be thirty-six hundred dollars. I'll pay the whole thing in advance—and I'll expect some discount for that, because you'll be using my money. See what sort of deal I can get from the owner, and if I like it you'll get everything up front."

"You have a bank account here in town?" Lombard felt that he was in a situation beyond his control. He had to try and get hold of it.

"That's my business. If we go ahead you'll be paid in cash." Outside the office, Peter Daniels nodded his head at the blue van, where the woman sat patiently waiting. "You drive slow, and we'll follow you along."

He swung up to the driver's seat. Lombard stood there in the road for a moment, looking up at him.

"How soon would you want to take possession—if you like it, I mean. It's empty now."

Daniels looked down at him, dark eyes expressionless. The woman had not even turned her head to Lombard.

"We're here now, and we have all our things with us." Daniels began to close the window. "We'll want immediate possession—today."

The first thing that Otis Lombard did with the money was to take it over to Jack Carswell at the police station in Thurmont. Thirty-four bills, each for a hundred dollars, made a small packet on the Chief's desk. After a while he pushed them back to Lombard.

"Not hot, Otis, far as we can tell. And real money, too. What's the problem? Some people don't trust banks, you know that. You think he's a troublemaker of some kind?"

"I don't know." Lombard took a deep breath and wriggled in his chair. "If I give you a good description of him, could you run a check on that, too?"

"Easy. Getting nervous in your old age? What makes you think he may be a bad 'un?"

"Dunno. Maybe he's not. Not with any sort of a record, anyway. I just can't get over the way he looks and talks. You know, he had his woman—wife or whatever she is—too beat down to speak when we went over to Tantalon Farm. I don't know if she liked it or not, she never said one word."

"Can't do anything about that, Otis. Look, you think maybe you've got a little case of conscience?"

"What do you mean?" Lombard shifted again on the hard chair. "I've done nothing wrong, just tried to rent the property."

"You've put Daniels into Tatalon Farm, right? You know the local reputation of the place since Jensen died there. Sure, the death was an accident, I know that. I wonder if maybe you need to prove Daniels is a wrong one, though, so whatever happens you don't need to worry about him."

"That's nonsense."

"All right, all right, just a thought." Carswell leaned back in his chair. "So long as you're happy. As for the woman, we can't do a thing about that. If he's married to her or if he's not, there's no case for us there. I've told you the money's all right, anything past that we have to wait and see if we get any complaints. Let 'em move in, see how they behave. She's quiet, but I can't charge either of them for being quiet. Damn, I just wish more people were. You come on back here when you've got something real. I think this hot weather's boiling your brains a bit too much."

Summer was turning slowly to fall. It began to look as though Chief Jack Carswell was right. Tantalon Farm's new residents had moved in, and that was about all that anybody in town could say about them. Once a week, the woman drove into town for supplies. She was a tall blonde about twenty-five years old, and she spoke to no one beyond the minimal amount called for in her shopping. The mailman delivered an assortment of gun magazines to the farm, and no personal correspondence.

Otis Lombard had to make one visit to Tantalon Farm. There had been a complaint from across the river, that somebody had been firing high velocity rounds from a rifle.

Daniels met Lombard at the gate, just past the point where the dog could stretch his chain. It was a huge mongrel, an eighty-five pound mixture of Alsatian and mastiff. When Daniels was there, it was quiet and obedient, but the mailman told Lombard that he would never try and deliver to the house when the dog was alone. It had a quiet patience and waiting look that was more scary than any amount of wild barking.

Daniels listened to Lombard's recitation of the complaint from across the river, nodded once, and turned to go back to the house. There was no discussion, no excuses, and no promise to stop using high-velocity ammunition. On the other hand, Lombard received no more complaints from across the river.

No one in the town seemed to have much interest in Daniels and his woman. After a couple of months, as the leaves shrivelled to browns and reds and yellows, Lombard took his worries to Dr. Marsden. Tom Marsden was the town's only doctor, and a relative of the owner of Tantalon Farm. He was in his early thirties, a man who understood quietness very well himself. He had never married, never had an affair that anyone could point to in the County. Lombard told him everything that he knew about Daniels—little enough at that.

"The lease calls for property inspection twice a year, Tom. I wonder if you'd like to do it. You have old Jimmy's power of attorney up here."

"I do. But why not you? You're the real estate agent for the place. You did the lease."

Lombard shrugged his fatty shoulders. They sat there in silence for a while in Marsden's office, until Lombard looked questioningly at Tom Marsden.

"No, I won't do it. You're paranoid, Otis. Why should I go there and disturb them, when they keep to themselves and don't trouble anybody?"

"Well, you know the stories. When old Jensen—"

"You believe any of that? Drop it, Otis. You ought

to have better things to occupy your mind."

Tom Marsden had ended it there. Then the woman had come to see him at his office.

It was a dull, rainy day, with the first hint of colder weather in it. She sat in his waiting room, an old brown raincoat over her long-sleeved green blouse and faded orange skirt. When Tom called her in, the first thing that he noticed was her height. She matched him eye to eye, even in her flat heels. Near to six feet without shoes, and thinner than she ought to be. And pale, pale as a seedling that has never seen the sun.

She had trouble talking. With eyes downcast, she answered his questions in short and broken phrases. Donna Anselm. Never married. Twenty-seven years old. For two weeks now, she had been bleeding.

"Bleeding where?"

She lifted tortured grey eyes. Down here. A pale hand touched her lower abdomen for a second, then fluttered up to hide her mouth.

"All right." Tom sounded as positive and cheerful as he could. "First thing, Donna, I need to have a good look at you. Go on into the back room and take off your clothes. Put one of the white robes on. I'll be with you in a couple of minutes."

She did not move.

"Come on now, Donna." He stood in front of her. "What's the matter?"

"I—I don't want to take my clothes off." The gray eyes were a little reddened, as though she had been weeping before she came to the office. "Can you do it without that? Please?"

With her hands clasped in front of her, she was pleading, submissive. Tom Marsden felt the stirring of a strong new emotion; a dark excitement.

"I can't help you without an examination, Donna. I have to see for myself. You go back there, now, and get ready. I promise you, it will be quick, and I won't hurt you. Remember, I examine people all the time."

His voice was strong and forceful. She bowed her head, picked up her raincoat, and walked through to the rear office.

The examination took only five minutes. They were in the back room for more than twenty. The cause of the bleeding was obvious enough and easily treated, but now Tom knew why she did not want him to examine her. Donna Anselm's body was long and thin, with beautifully shaped arms and legs. Her skin was impossibly white, translucent and flawless. Tom should have been blasé about all forms of the human body. Instead he thought of a morning snowfield, before bird or animal moves to destroy the perfection. And he had trouble completing his examination. For on that snowfield, like the first flowers of spring, pale mauve and yellow crocuses bloomed. He saw the fading bruise marks of thumb and fingers blossoming on her delicate thighs and on the curve of her sloping shoulders. His hands trembled as he touched the stethoscope to her back and breast, and he had to force his mind again and again to concentrate on the examination.

When she had gone, he called Otis Lombard. He had changed his mind.

The inspection of the house, two days later, was a formality. Peter Daniels and Donna (mainly, Tom suspected, it was the latter) kept the house spotless. Even the old furniture had been neatly repaired, the splits in the sofa sewn and patched. The dirt floor of the basement had been carefully swept and levelled. Tom stopped for a moment at the old pump. Donna primed it by hand, then switched on the electric motor. The water was slightly effervescent and tasted pleasantly of dissolved mineral salts.

Tom smiled at her. "It's been a long time since I tasted that—twenty years or more. It's as good as ever. I bet you could bottle it and sell it."

She looked back at him quietly. He realized that she had no social conversation.

"No more problems with the bleeding?"

She shook her head. "It's all better. Did you tell—"

"Nobody. I'll have to have a word with Mr. Daniels, though. All right?"

She looked troubled. "He's out in the woods at the back, with Wilson." She saw Tom's confused look. "Wilson's the dog. They're off hunting."

"I'll find them." He smiled at her. "There's no need for you to come out, Donna. It's been nice seeing you again. Remember, now"—his voice took on a stern and professional tone—"you must keep taking those pills, when the instructions tell you to. And you call me or come and see me as soon as you begin to run low on them."

He left the farm house by the back door, walking to where the ground sloped slowly lower, northwards towards the river. Up near the road the fall air had been clear and still, so the smoke of Tom's cigar rose straight and blue. As he walked downhill he could feel the change. The air currents began to turn and vary, puffs of breeze sweeping in first from one side, then from another. He could see no sign of Peter Daniels, but as he came into the denser trees there was a sudden terrifying growl about twenty yards in front of him. A huge dog burst from the brush and ran straight at him, jaws wide.

"Wilson. Down." The shout came just before the dog was leaping on him. It dropped to its belly on the earth. Tom had frozen, forearms up to protect his throat. After a tense second Daniels came out from the bushes. His round face was expressionless and he carried a twenty-two rifle under his left arm.

"Don't ever come back here on you own, 'less you tell me you'll be coming." His voice was flat and toneless. "He's been trained to protect this property and he'll do it. What are you doing here? Lombard told me you'd be coming to look over the house, the way it says in the lease—not the rest of the land."

"I saw the house." Tom gestured at the dog, where it lay quivering with excitement. "Call him off. He doesn't look safe."

"He's safe enough. Wilson, heel. So what the hell are you doing back here, anyway?"

He crouched down into a squatting position and pulled a cigarette from his jacket pocket. As he tried to light it, Tom noticed that the wind moved around the smoke, so that the flame was frustrated until Daniels had it completely shielded with his hands.

"I wanted to talk to you about Donna. She may not have told you this, but a few weeks ago she had a miscarriage."

"The bleeding?" Daniels looked thoughtful. "Damn that woman. I saw blood on her clothes, but I thought it came from something else. No, she didn't tell me she'd been pregnant. But what about it?"

"I gave her some medication. She'll recover all right, but I wanted to tell you about it, so that you will . . . I mean, so that she'll be able to recover quietly and not have anything that will make her . . ."

"You tryin' to tell me something?" Daniels drew on his cigarette. "Look here, Mister, you came here to inspect the property. All right, that's in the lease. I don't think the lease includes telling me how I ought to run my life. So if there's nothing new, why don't you get the hell out of here? I'll look after Donna."

Tom stood his ground. "She's not a strong woman, you ought to know that."

Daniels flicked a quick look at the dog, lying on its stomach next to him. "Yeah, I know. She's a sickly one. Think maybe I ought to throw her out, get me a new one?"

Tom fumbled in his pocket for another cigar. He had dropped the other one when the dog attacked. "No. That's not my business. I'm only concerned about her health. Look, don't misunderstand me." His voice was gruff but conciliatory. "I'm not trying to stick my nose in where it's not wanted, but I am a doctor and she's a patient. That's all I care about, and I'd do the same for anybody else."

He tried, unsuccessfully, to light his cigar with a wooden match. Daniels watched his efforts with a flat grin. "You'll never do it that way. Here." He held out his lighter. "Place of the what's it called?"

"Meeting Place of the Winds."

"Right, it lives up to it too. I've never been here when there wasn't a set of cross-currents in the air. Watch this." He held up his cigarette. Little streamers of smoke ran first one way, then the other. Tom shielded his cigar and the flame, and finally managed to get it to draw. He nodded his thanks and handed back the lighter. He cleared his throat.

"How's the hunting here? Up to what you expected?"

"Fine." Daniels showed real animation for the first time. "I've never seen so much game in one place. Possum, raccoons, squirrels, rabbits, even deer. I wouldn't be surprised to get a bear one day. This place ever been hunted before?"

"Not really." Tom paused. "Before the last tenant, the old man who had this place kept it as a sort of wild life sanctuary, didn't hunt at all. Had it for forty years or so. He claimed that it had been a sort of holy place for the Indians, way back when. You noticed how tame the animals are?"

"Were." Daniels grinned and ground out his cigarette in the earth. "We've changed that a bit, me and Wilson. Watch now. I don't get as much accuracy with these as with the high-velocity rounds, but I guess it's more of a challenge that way. Hold real still for a couple of minutes. You don't need to worry about that cigar, they're not used to that."

He lifted the rifle to his shoulder. It was a Ruger 10-22 carbine, a ten chamber semi-automatic. Tom noticed that Daniels was firing it left-handed.

The men stood silently for about a minute, while the breezes of the woods swirled and tugged about them. Finally there was a flicker of movement in one of the trees about thirty yards north of them. Daniels sighted carefully and fired one round. The moment that the rifle was fired, Wilson was off through the woods, head low. A second later there was a growl and a high-pitched scream.

Tom waited. The dog did not reappear.

"Won't he retrieve?"

"If I want him to." Daniels was looking down at his rifle. "That was just a squirrel. I'll have him bring back deer or bear. The small stuff is his."

"Did you get a clean hit there? I thought I heard something on the ground."

Daniels looked up, eyes narrow. "Clean hit? Man, let me tell you, at this range I never miss. I didn't aim for the body. With varmints like squirrel and possum I aim for a back leg, a back foot if I can get a sight on it. That brings 'em out of the tree, and it lets Wilson have a bit of fun. He'll tear 'em apart while they're still alive and running."

He was smiling, fondling his rifle. Tom licked his lips. "You're really into hunting, aren't you? Did you ever try big game? You might get a black bear around here if you're lucky, but you'll never see anything like the real stuff. Grizzlies start further west."

"And they're protected, eh? Guess we don't worry us too much about that. Some day, when I can go back—" He broke off abruptly, as though too much had already been said. "Big game? I've been after big game already."

He squatted down again, laying the rifle carefully on the ground, flat against the surface. From a pocket of his jacket he pulled out an old black pouch of finely oiled leather. He unfolded it carefully and held it out to Tom.

"Take a look at these. You ought to be able to recognize 'em, I'd think."

Tom looked at the collection of misshapen pearls,

white and gleaming. He drew in his breath. "Teeth. Human teeth, by the look of them."

"Damn right. Picked these up over in Vietnam. Big game, eh? Every one I shot, I took a tooth. Couldn't do it sometimes, of course, when we were backing up, but I got forty-five of them before I was shipped out."

Tom picked out an incisor and peered at it closely. "What about this one? You didn't get it over there. It has a metal filling in it."

Daniels was smiling, his black button eyes glittering with pleasure. "You got good eyes, Doc, but I got it in Nam all right. There was some things there that needs shooting a lot more than any of your gooks." He laughed. "Bit of a come down, eh? After all that, I'm out here shooting possum."

Tom looked at him quietly. "You need it, don't you?"

"Reckon I do. Better to be doing this, though, than maybe be up at the top of the old Texas Tower." He suddenly shivered. "Me and old Wilson, we've come a long way."

He was struck by another thought and turned to look towards the river. When he looked back his face was grim. "All right, so you've seen the property. You can let me worry about Donna, there'll be no medical problems there. And let me know if you ever decide to go off and look for grizzly. I'd be taking a risk, but maybe it'd be worth it."

He whistled. A few seconds later Wilson came trotting back through the scrub. He was grinning, long jaws agape and bloodied. Tom looked at the dog warily, then turned back towards the house. Before he was out of sight, he turned again to Daniels.

"None of my business again, but why'd you call him Wilson?"

Daniels grinned. Side by side, dog and man seemed a good match. "I reckon you already guessed it. For my old platoon leader, the son of a bitch. Meanest man you ever saw, and the blackest coon in the army." He patted his pocket. "Number twenty-nine, he was."

Tom nodded. "Watch out for those squirrels. Some of them are supposed to be rabid."

He headed back to the road and his car, skirting the house. Inside, he fancied he could see the pale shadow of Donna at one of the windows. He felt his heart pounding savagely as he climbed back into his silver Pontiac. It was a couple of minutes before he could calm himself enough to drive back to town.

The next inspection of the property would be scheduled for March. By that time there ought to be real crocuses blooming on Tantalon's snowy slopes.

Long before March, Dr. Tom Marsden had found reasons to visit Tantalon Farm. The first time it was the delivery of a prescription—"to save you the trouble of a trip into town." Then there was a request from the power company for permission to clear-cut along the common boundary of their properties. After that, in late November, it was a turkey as a surprise gift from the owner down in Florida. He had invested the thirty-four hundred from the Tantalon lease and made fifty percent on the money. Now he wanted to boast about it.

Peter Daniels accepted the visits with cynical

amusement, but after the first one he seemed to welcome them. He sat with Tom in the long, dark livingroom and talked about hunting. The flat, factual descriptions excited Tom Marsden profoundly in a way he could not control or describe. While they talked, Donna moved around the house like a pale ghost. Tom secretly admired her fine honey-blond hair and graceful movement as she served the two men with strong coffee and cheap, rough brandy. She never spoke. The long-sleeved dresses and full skirts hid her fragile beauty and white skin. Daniels noticed Tom's covert glances, but never mentioned it. That too was a source of some black vein of quirkish humor.

As the fall wore on, the winds about the old house grew stronger. They seemed to be moving up from the valley bottom, every day a little higher and a little more forceful. They called back the old stories about the property, from the time before Tantalon Farm had been built. Tom had explained the legend to Daniels, the tale of Indian spirits and wind-devils. Daniels showed no interest. He laughed when he heard Jensen's story about the winds learning from the people in the house. Jensen had been very old when he died. Even Tom found the tale ridiculous when he told it and deliberately changed to a self-mocking tone before he reached the end.

He left as Peter Daniels was putting on his coat. There was an extra handful of cartridges stuffed in the pocket. Daniels thought he had seen a bear down by the stream the previous evening. It had been too big for a raccoon and it seemed to merge into the darkness in a way that no deer could match.

Daniels walked the woods for many hours without

catching any further sign of the bear. Those first days of December were bringing a change to Tantalon Farm. Fog filled the hollow down near the water, and the leafless trees offered less resistance to the veering winds. The old wooden house was well-built and warm inside, but somehow the eaves would catch the north wind that whistled across the lowland. There was a constant sighing around the walls, a moan of air moving under the low-hung eaves.

Donna made fewer visits to the town. She spent most of the day at the north-facing window, looking out for signs of Daniels and Wilson as they prowled the woods together. She was not a reader, but the old bookcases held one volume that had caught her attention as she was cleaning the room. As she sat by the window, sewing buttons and patches on ripped blouses and nightgowns, she popped it open in front of her. The book told an assortment of Indian legends of the Northeast. Donna's education had stopped in the fifth grade, when her mother had pulled her from school to travel the roads of West Virginia. Now she sat there, mouthing the words to herself. Even when dusk advanced she did not bother to turn on the lights. She moved from her place only to cook their meals and to tend the log fire that Daniels insisted should be kept blazing in the living room, regardless of the central heating.

He came back to the house only when it was fully dark. His eyes were full of an excited light that they never showed during the day. After dinner he fed Wilson himself — his only household chore — then sat silently with the dog at his feet. Until they went to bed he would obsessively clean his rifles, his eyes following

Donna as she moved about the quiet house. He had not yet found his bear, but today he had seen spoor down by the edge of the stream.

Tom Marsden's worry for Donna's miscarriage were now quite unnecessary. Some other fever had gripped Peter Daniels. Donna's skin was unblemished, unmarked by the pastel bloom of soft bruises. The couple slept together, but Donna had less and less reason to repair her torn garments.

The first snow came two weeks before Christmas. It fell in a smooth blanket over the town and the roads but at Tantalon it swirled and drifted, borne into random heaps and delicate wind-shaped traceries on banks and hedges.

That afternoon Peter Daniels came home elated through the snowy darkness. He had seen more tracks of the bear, rambling their way higher out of the valley and ranging up closer to the house.

The dog shared Daniels' excitement. Instead of lying quietly by the fire after dinner, it paced about the house, ears pricked up and fur bristling.

"Can you get him to sit? He makes me nervous." Donna was sitting by the fire, listening to a country and western show on the old tube radio she had found in the basement. It worked well, but pulled in only three stations.

Peter Daniels ignored her request. "Dammit, I wish that Tom Marsden was here. I know he'd be real interested in this. You should've seen that spoor, he's a *big* one."

He began to pace like the dog. Already he and Donna had spoken enough words for a month of evenings.

"I'll take the twenty-two," he went on. "But I'll take the high-velocity shells. Did you ever see one of those fellers when he's injured?"

She looked up from her battered book, face vacant. Usually he gave brief orders, get this, do that. She had never heard him this way before.

"He'll get mean if I just hit him in the leg." Daniel's eyes were moving in his head, sweeping from one side of the room to the other. His voice was breathy and absorbed. "I've seen an old brown bear that was hit that way. Just a young 'un, but he ripped the guts clean out of a big fighting Doberman that came in too close. Don't want that happenin' to old Wilson, I've got to take that s.o.b. clean and right or not do it at all. Through the eye, or in the middle of the throat."

"Big storm coming," she said, when he paused by the window. His loquacity moved her to speak. "I heard it on the radio here. Tomorrow, they say. High winds and cold, and more snow. We'll get high winds and snow by afternoon."

"Yeah." He was peering out of the window, listening to the breathy moan of the wind. Wilson had moved over to the door and stood by it, stiff-legged and bristling. His growl was deep in his chest, defiant and angry.

Daniels rubbed at the fog on the inside of the window pane. "Let's see, for cold weather, wind'll be from the north and west. That ought to bring him this way, more'n likely. He won't want to walk into the wind. Wonder what he weighs? Seems to me one of them books ought to tell me a way to get an idea how big he is from his footprints."

He went off to the kitchen where his books and

magazines were kept. The house was quiet again except for the steadily rising wind and the unhappy growl of Wilson, padding from door to door. The wind in the eaves muttered unsteadily, all broken whistles and deep sighs. Donna stood up to put another log on the fire. When she sat down again she picked up her book. It opened as usual to one story, an old Indian tale that she read again and again. Her mouth made the word sounds as she ran again over the familiar lines. Outside, the wind began to veer north and west.

Winter storms in that part of the country are never predictable, no matter how much confidence the forecasters display. Instead of high winds, by the following afternoon the air had become completely still. There was an absolute calm, with a slate-grey snow sky overhead and no sounds from birds or animals when Daniels and Wilson set out for the river. Wilson was excited, wagging his tail, growling, starting again and again after unseen and non-existent prey.

They walked the property from side to side, from end to end. Even the eternal cross-currents in the bottom land were stilled. The stream surface looked oily and sullen, a lifeless slither of glycerine.

Daniels had ignored the rare small game that they saw. As the afternoon wore into evening, however, he angrily put a bullet into a squirrel. He watched with satisfaction as it fell screaming from the tree, its right hind leg shot away. Wilson seemed to sense that they were after much bigger game. The dog did not plunge away after the wounded squirrel in his usual way. Instead, he looked up for a moment then continued a steady quartering of the ground, seeking some elusive and shifting scent.

It was dark before five. Daniels came in through the back door and went to the kitchen. For two hours he hunched there silently, a bottle of bourbon open on the table beside him. His rifle, still loaded with a full chamber, leaned against his chair. Donna tiptoed about the house, placing his meal in front of him without speaking and cleaning up as quietly as she could. His eyes followed her when he thought she was not looking, and now and again he would touch his rifle. The level in the bottle of bourbon fell steadily.

At eight o'clock, the wind began again. It was more savage than before, a screaming fury around the walls of the house. With it came the snow. With the rattle of hail and the whistle of cold air, there was a chattering and a screaming noise like a vast horde of angry animals. By ten o'clock, the house was banked deeper in drifted snow and the windows were whited over.

Donna had kept the fire burning bright. The inside of the house was warm and comfortable, but Wilson was again restless. He prowled from door to door, growling unhappily. Finally he came to a halt by the door that led out to the northern woods. He began to bark madly. His lips had drawn back from his white fangs and he stood on his hind legs and scrabbled furiously at the wooden door.

Daniels came from the kitchen, his rifle in his hand. He was breathing heavily. Without a look at Donna he went to the door and opened it, peering out through the glass of the storm door at the dark blizzard.

"What is it, boy? What you see out there?"

Wilson growled and yelped, throwing himself

against the stout glass. He was looking at something down the slope, beyond the edge of the clearing.

"Get my coat." Daniels sounded relieved as he snapped the words to Donna and rubbed the smooth barrel of the rifle. "It's the bear. He's out there, I know it. Wilson can scent him. Now I'll get him, when he comes near the house like this." He was filling his pocket with cartridges, more spare rounds than he would ever need. As he turned to grab his coat from her, the dog threw itself wildly against the door again. The restraining catch broke under the force of the flying body. Barking madly, Wilson plunged out into the swirling darkness.

"Stay." Daniels' shout was lost in the wind. "Damn it, he's off. Where is he, boy? Where's he hiding?"

With his coat still unbuttoned, Daniels grabbed up his rifle and flashlight and opened the door. He was swallowed up immediately in the roaring darkness.

Donna stood shivering at the door for a few minutes, then became too cold to wait longer. She left the door unlocked and went back to the fire to warm her frozen hands. After a few minutes she picked up her book of stories and sat down patiently to wait.

Outside, the wind was still strengthening. It howled and raged around the house, louder and louder, blotting out all other sounds.

The winter storm lasted for thirty-six hours, driving home its message of freezing violence. When it died, it died suddenly. The first man out on the road to Tantalon Farm was the mailman, carrying out his old pledge to deliver whatever the conditions.

He got as far as the gate of the farm with his gun

magazines, then thought twice about his promise. This called for more than a willingness to face bad weather. As he put his hand on the latch, a black streak of savagery had hurled itself at him from the other side. He backed away quickly. The dog was foaming at the mouth, with bloodied muzzle and slavering fangs. The mailman looked up towards the house. A pale face was peering at him out of the window, and a white hand waved for help.

He was back two hours later with Tom Marsden and Jack Carswell. The Police Chief had been over from Thurmont, checking the state of the plowed roads, and he was still in town when Marsden called on him for help. It took two bullets from his thirty-eight to silence Wilson. Then the three men walked round to the back door of the house. The torn body of Peter Daniels lay there, half-buried by the drifted snow. His hands, arms and throat showed the marks of a terrible struggle for life.

"You've got to get her out of here without seeing this." Carswell nodded to the body, then jerked his head towards the house.

"I'll look after that. I'll take her into town through the front door. Let me take a quick look at the body." He bent over Daniels for a couple of minutes, leaving the Police Chief to support the sick and shaking mailman.

"All right, not much doubt about that." Marsden straightened up. "I'll get her out of here."

Carswell was shaking his head. "Funny thing, this. The old man lived in this place for forty-odd years, and never a sign of trouble. Wonder how he did it. Maybe you ought to write to him down in Florida and ask."

"Maybe. Tantalon has done it again, though." Tom Marsden rubbed his hands on clean snow. "Now I don't know who'll come and live here. You'd better get me a sample from that dog while your men are here. It did a real job on Daniels. Take a look at those wounds. Dog must have been rabid as hell."

The other two men bent low, drawn by the old fascination of death. The mailman shuddered and stood up hurriedly.

Tom Marsden took Donna away from the old farmhouse and gave her a temporary lodging in the apartment behind his doctor's waiting-room. His official report on Daniels' death was never questioned: attacked by a maddened dog that must have been bitten by a rabid squirrel on one of their hunting expeditions.

The town forgot quickly as it fought its way through an unusually savage winter. In late February, Tom Marsden married Donna Anselm.

Marsden's test had found no sign of rabies in the dog. That was never reported. In March the Marsdens moved into Tantalon Farm. Tom began to prowl the spring woods, carrying Peter Daniels' old rifle through the swirling cross-currents of wind.

Inside the walls of the old house, sheilded from the eyes of any curious outsider, the crocuses were blossoming again on the hidden snowfields.

The Belfrey
By James Anderson

Why didn't the watchman warn them about the old mill?

The Belfrey

by James Anderson

It was late afternoon when the blue Pontiac pulled into the deserted parking lot of the Dodgeville Dye Works. The ancient towers and belfreys of the mill cast long shadows over the sleepy town. Dave Walsh yawned as he climbed from the passenger's seat and looked at the building.

It was a typical textile mill. The building must have been two centuries old. Its sprawling brick walls were crumbling away in places and the largest belfrey sported a huge gaping hole, as if it had been blown apart from the inside. Dave was tired and in no mood to begin a job this late in the day. If he had been alone he would surely have left; but he knew the boss would never leave a job behind — not with the prospect of regaining an old customer at stake.

"You sure this is the place, Eddy?" he asked his boss.

"Accordin' ta the map it is," he replied. "Looks like a real dump."

"Sure does. Have you been here before?"

"Who's there?" he asked.

"We're here ta file a frame. Tenter frame number three. From the Winsor Company."

"Oh yeah. The Winsor Company. The boss finisher called ya earlier."

"Yeah. I'm Eddy and this is my partner Dave."

"Pleased ta meet ya. Name's Tom. Come on. I'll show you to the frame."

They followed the man through the musty corridors, past huge vats of dye and antique textile machinery.

The guard's hand was bandaged tightly from fingers to wrist. The gauze covering still oozed with pus and blood.

"What happened ta yer hand?" Eddy asked.

"Ah . . . nothing. I just . . . ah . . . cut it on some broken glass."

"Too bad. Hey, they still got wild cats here?"

"No, not like before. They still got cats ta chase the mice but they're not as mean. They're on the second floor, usually. Just don't try ta pet 'em. They're not your typical house cat."

"Thanks for the advice."

"The bathroom's this way," the guard said, pointing down a deserted corridor, "and there's a coffee machine upstairs. The frame's over here. It's in rough shape."

Eddy examined the chain quickly.

"I've seen worse. What's it, a ninety footer?"

"Yup. This one's a ninety. The rest are eighty."

"Looks like we get the prize," Dave muttered.

"We won't be outta here in less than ten hours by the looks of this one," Eddy said.

Dave groaned. He'd already put in an eight hour shift at the shop. They'd be lucky to finish by two in the morning. Damn this mill for calling them at such an hour! They could surely have waited until morning. And Dave did have his own work to do.

It was the curse of the times that college graduates were forced to do menial labor to earn a living, he thought. He'd been lied to. Ever since he was a child they'd told him to get an education. It was the only way to make it in the world. He'd believed them. He'd worked his way through college, struggling for his degree, and then had been unable to find a job. He played at graduate school for a while, then married and took on a menial job with a textile machine company. The pay wasn't bad, but Dave found it difficult to accept his role of punching a time clock with his degree in English behind him. He'd taken to free-lance writing, with some success, but the sporadic checks were not enough. So he worked and hated every minute of it.

He opened his tool chest and prepared his files while Eddy searched for a place to set up the flourescent lights. The security guard took his leave and continued his rounds.

Dave hated these road jobs with a passion. He'd turned down the last six in a row and it really was his turn to go. He couldn't back out this time.

"Hey buddy, ya all set?"

"Just about, Eddy. Did you get the lights hooked up?"

"Sure did. Now let's see." He took a set of files that Dave had prepared. "I'll take the far side."

The older man climbed under the frame and adjusted his light. Dave often wondered where his partner found his endless reserve of energy. He was pushing retirement age yet looked not a day over fifty. When Dave was exhausted from a long day's work, Eddy was ready for eight hours more.

With a sigh, Dave adjusted his own light and looked underneath the blades of the tenter chain. The blades were dulled by years of use. This would be one rough job, he thought.

"We give it fifteen rubs," Eddy said.

That meant they had to rub the file across each link of the chain fifteen times before they could even begin to file the thing. That would sharpen the blades. Since it was a ninety footer, there were over a thousand links in the chain.

In theory the machine would take a roll of cloth that was, say, two hundred inches wide and stretch it through an oven to a width of maybe two hundred and ten inches. The links on either side that composed the chain grabbed the cloth in their blade-like jaws and pulled, stretching it as the distance between the chains increased. Unless these blades were *very* sharp, the cloth would slip out and not stretch. It was Dave's job to make sure this did not happen.

They began their work, almost forgetting their dismal surroundings in their labor. They would file a couple dozen links, then Eddy would engage the power and move the chain forward slowly. The

86

finished section would move around and into the still-hot oven while the unfinished ones would emerge from the oven to be filed. They worked steadily for about three-quarters of an hour and Eddy criticized the work, the management of the company, politicians, and the Boston Red Sox, all in no particular order. Finally, Eddy stopped for a break.

"I'm going to the bathroom," Eddy said. "Want a coffee?"

"No thanks. I'll wait here."

"Sure. Why don't ya read for a while? I'll be right back."

Dave decided to take Eddy's suggestion. He reached into his bag of belongings and took out his book. He was rereading *Dracula*. Looking at his surroundings in the dismal mill he wished he'd brought along something by Walt Disney.

He read a chapter, sitting in a corner of the old mill with his feet propped up on a stool. When he was done with the chapter he put the book down; Eddy should be back any minute. He should have been back already, Dave reflected, but he knew Eddy well enough by now. He had probably met the security guard in the men's room and they were sitting there throwing the bull about wild cats. Then Eddy would tell him about the wonderful job the Winsor Company did manufacturing new chains, hoping that the guard would say something to the boss finisher. Dave laughed to himself. That was how his company sold fifty percent of its new tenter chains, he thought.

Dave looked at his watch. It was 5:45 and dark outside. He sat back and tried to relax, hoping Eddy would hurry up so they could get this job finished and get home before it was *too* late. Good thing it was Friday, Dave thought; he'd never be able to drag himself out of bed at six o'clock tomorrow. He closed his eyes for just an instant, then lost the desire to open them again. The last thing he remembered before falling asleep was the uncanny stillness of the air.

Dave awoked feeling as if he had slept for hours. He looked around; there was still no sign of Eddy. He glanced at his watch. It read nine fifty three. He had slept for over four hours! It was impossible! Where was Eddy? Jesus Christ, we'll never get out of here now, Dave thought.

He stood up and shook off his drowsiness. He'd better find Eddy. The frame was in the same position as when he'd fallen asleep, so Eddy hadn't returned since then. Where the Hell could the bastard be?

He headed for the men's room. Dave vaguely remembered the directions. Making his way through the shadows and past the huge oven that housed the frame they were working on, Dave found the corridor leading to the bathroom. Perhaps Eddy had become ill. Maybe the poor bastard had passed out over the toilet or something—he might even have had a heart attack! Feeling more than a little guilty, Dave entered the men's room.

"Eddy? You in here?"

No answer.

He checked each of the stalls to be sure. They were empty, except for the usual collection of graffiti.

"Eddy?" he called, louder this time. His words echoed hollowly and returned with no reply.

"Jesus Christ," he said out loud. "I hope he didn't

fall down the stairs or something."

Dave remembered Eddy asking if he wanted a coffee. The machine was on the second floor. Dave decided he'd better go downstairs and look for Eddy, but not until he'd returned to the toolbox for a flashlight.

Dave retraced his steps to the frame they'd been working on. The area was still deserted. He'd hoped Eddy would be back and waiting for him. That would have been too easy, he thought, opening the toolbox and taking out the flashlight. When he even thought of venturing to the second floor of the mill his heart pounded in protest. It was true that Dave wrote about heroic characters who had more courage than brains, but his own quest for adventure lay behind a typewriter. He would let his characters do the work while he sat back and watched. It would be much easier if he found the security guard, he mused. With that in mind he returned to the main door.

He searched a few darkened corridors before finding the guard's booth. It was encased in glass and equipped with a desk, chair, and telephone. It was unoccupied. So much for that idea, he thought. Dave scribbled a note and placed it on the desk, just in case the guard should return.

He decided to check out the rest of the bottom floor before going upstairs. Maybe he would find the guard after all. The main corridors were dimly-lit — the smaller ones were completely dark. The flashlight barely pierced the blackness between the machinery.

Dave searched quickly but thoroughly. When he passed the far end of the machine they'd been working on he checked the spaces between it and the other frames just in case Eddy had fallen on his way back. There was nothing.

The place was chilly now that the sun had set, and the surroundings looked more bleak than ever. Just as he turned away from the tenter frame it came to life and the chain began to move. He heard the distinct crash of the flourescent lights breaking ninety feet away.

"Eddy!" he called. "Where the Hell are you?"

Dave ran to the far end of the frame, fully expecting to see Eddy moving the chain. When he arrived there was no one in sight. The oven switched on with a roar and spit hot air from either end while the chain gained speed. The lights, which had been resting on the chain, had crashed to the floor and shattered into a thousand pieces.

"Jesus Christ," Dave said out loud. He was a writer of the supernatural but he didn't actually *believe* in such nonsense. The security guard must have hit the "on" switch by mistake. Either that or there was a short in the wiring. Dave climbed over the toolbox and shut the thing off with a curse.

Now the lights were ruined and there was still no sign of Eddy.

Gathering his nerves together as best he could, Dave set off in the direction of the men's room again. Eddy must be upstairs.

Swallowing hard, Dave entered the dark corridor leading to the farthest side of the mill. He was still a bit shook up about the machine coming on by itself. It must have been a short. Electricity did some strange things at times, he thought.

Dave carefully followed the flashlight beam as it

traced is path over the ancient floorboards. The worn oak actually bent with his weight as he walked over it. Dave passed roll upon roll of cloth, hundreds of yards of fabric in various stages of finishing. Mice scurried before his light and hid between the mountains of cloth.

After what seemed like hours of following the same endless corridor, Dave ran into a dead end. A steep flight of stairs led upwards, toward an open trapdoor on the ceiling. A dim light shone from this opening.

He had searched the entire bottom floor. Though he loathed the thought of going upstairs there was nothing else to do. Slowly and very carefully he climbed the steep staircase. The flimsy railing shook unsteadily with every step.

Dave swore to himself and wished Eddy had left *him* the keys to the car. Damned if he wouldn't get the hell out of this godawful mill and leave Eddy to his own devices. The thought of spending the night in this hellhole was too much.

He peeked his head through the trapdoor and flashed his light into the shadows. Several large rats scattered at the beam. He waited until the rats were gone before climbing from the stairway and onto the second floor. He wished he had a gun, or even a knife, but how was he to know he'd need a weapon to do a routine job in a textile mill? At any rate, he didn't like the looks of the rats.

"Well," he thought. "This'll make a great story if I ever get out of this dump."

He stood still for a moment and allowed himself a leisurely view of the place. The second floor was much like the first; if anything, it was even more dismal.

The floorboards were certainly weaker and the lighting was worse. Spare parts littered the area. He recognized several chains, a couple of dismantled ovens, some tenter rails, and several boxes of assorted gears, driveshafts, and motors. The chemical smell was gone, replaced by the overpowering stench of the rats. An occasional light was turned on full. The remaining overhead lights refused to respond to any switch that Dave pressed.

There was only one direction to walk—a blank wall stared at his rear. Slowly he pressed forward, wishing he was home with his wife, sharing a nice warm cup of tea, and then a nice warm bed. . . .

His watch read eleven o'clock. He'd been searching for over an hour. Instead of being almost finished with the frame, they'd hardly begun.

There were fewer lights as Dave continued his search. He stopped at a crate of spare parts and examined them carefully. He salvaged an iron pipe from the pile and hefted its weight. It would do.

Rats scattered before him as he continued and Dave felt a shudder run up his spine. He prayed that the rodents were well-fed.

He turned a corner and followed the corridor between shoulder-high rolls of rat-eaten fabric. Straight ahead, his light sparkled off a pair of bright green eyes.

Dave squinted into the shadows. It was a cat.

The thing was not exceptionally large, but what it lacked in size it more than made up for in rancor. It snarled and advanced toward him, stalking him confidently. Dave backed away and almost tripped on some gear casings. He crouched low and hefted the pipe again, waiting for the animal to spring. He did not wait long.

The cat vaulted through the air with an angry yowl, it's razor-sharp claws bared and aimed at Dave's exposed neck. Self preservation took control. Without thinking, Dave raised the pipe and swung it like a baseball bat. He felt the impact and heard the distinct crack of breaking bones. The cat screamed, an angry, painful scream that echoed through the old mill like the devil himself. Dave felt the skull split and he turned his lips up in a beastial grin. It was the ultimate joy of conquest, of taking the life of a hated foe, and the cat fell away from the pipe and crashed into a roll of cloth. Dave smashed it again, crushing the head into a bloody pulp. In death, the animal looked like a harmless kitten.

Dave brushed the dust from his clothes but the cat blood would not come out. He wished he could turn around and leave this place behind, leave Eddy and his damned job to the rats. But no. It was too late now. He'd come this far and would see the thing through, even if he had to battle more of the cats. His confidence increased by his victory, he finished his search of the second floor, grimly clutching his blood-stained pipe until his knuckles turned white.

When he reached the farthest end of the building he found another stairway. It led to the third floor.

He had no choice now. He ascended the stairs, wondering if Eddy waited for him, even now, on the first floor. It was too good to be true, he thought, and continued on his way.

Several drops of fresh blood stained the staircase ahead.

The stairs were steep and, like the first set, they were covered by a trap door at the ceiling. This door was shut.

Dave climbed the stairs slowly and held onto the weak railings for his very life. Carefully he pushed against the overhead door. It opened with a groan, as if it had been closed for years.

There was virtually no light on the third floor. Dave followed the trail of blood with his flashlight. Overhead he heard the squawk and squeak of hundreds of bats. When he looked up at the ceiling he could see the yellow glow of their malevolent eyes.

He shuddered and tried to think of something else. He dared not shine the light upwards, for that would only set the rodents flying. As frightening as the glowing eyes were hanging from the rafters, Dave preferred them on the ceiling to flying about.

The trail of blood was sporadic but easy to follow. Dave ignored the bats and continued his search. He passed several abandoned machines of all types and stopped at another staircase. This set of stairs was long and spiral. Dave shone his light upward along its length, frightening the bats to flight as he did so. He ducked and covered his head as the repulsive creatures flew past, their leathery wings brushing against his naked arms. Dave swallowed bile and remained still until they settled down.

Once the commotion had stopped Dave raised the light again. The stairway spiraled upward—to the tallest belfrey that he'd noticed from the outside! He couldn't imagine himself climbing those stairs. Yet the trail of blood—fresh blood—led to this tower, the one that seemed to have been blown apart from the inside.

Eddy might be up there hurt, or even dying, for all he knew. The man had always treated Dave right, often listening to his dreams and plans as they rode home after a long day's work. Eddy never made him work too hard, and always treated him to expensive meals at the company's expense whenever they were working on the road. Dave could never live with himself if anything happened to Eddy because of him. Right now, he was responsible for his boss.

Cursing himself for his goddamned conscience, Dave climbed the stairs to the belfrey.

The wood creaked with each step. Suddenly it gave; his foot crashed through the rotten wood and his ankle twisted painfully. Dave moaned but managed to keep from falling down the stairs. He eased himself back up, testing the injured leg. It was sore, but not seriously hurt.

When he reached the top he found a door, shut and bolted before him. Kneeling on the top stair, Dave took his bloody pipe and smashed the rusted bolt. The wood splintered and the door swung inward of its own accord.

Dave rubbed his injured ankle until he felt safe in putting his weight on it. Taking a deep breath he entered the upper belfrey.

His flashlight did little to dent the darkness until he turned around to face the gaping hole in the wall of the belfrey. Then he saw the full moon as it cast its mildewed shadows through the opening and into the darkened chamber. Bats chitted overhead and the floor was littered with their foul droppings. It was impossible for Eddy to be here, he thought. But what of the blood? Dave probed the darkness with his flashlight but found nothing.

Then, hanging over the edge of the gaping hole, he saw a hand. It seemed to be reaching inside, hanging on to the edge of the opening for its very life. Dave ran to it without hesitation.

"Eddy!" he called. "Hold on!"

He gripped the hand in his own, dropping the flashlight in his haste. He pulled. Only then did he realize the truth. The hand lifted up easily, dripping blood. The attached wrist had been severed from the arm.

Dave looked down in horror upon the thing he held on to. It seemed to clutch with a grip of its own, as if it still possessed the spark of life. Fresh blood poured from the arteries of the wrist, even as he held it. Then, as he gripped in in the moonlight and stared, Dave saw the wedding ring on the third finger. He recognized it immediately. It belonged to Eddy.

Dave forgot about his injured leg, forgot about the bats, even forgot about his flashlight as he dropped the grisley hand to the floor and ran from the tower, down the stairs and into the darkness of the third floor. He remembered the flashlight as he tripped past the machinery and debris. The bats, no longer held back by the flashlight, swooped and flew at his head.

Somehow he managed to find the stairs that led downstairs. He still clutched the pipe, swinging it overhead at the bats. He clubbed several of them before lowering himself down the staircase.

He took the stairs two at a time, breaking the railing just as he reached the floor. He continued running, disregarding any fear except that of the unknown evil in the belfrey. When he finally found the last set of stairs and reached the first floor he was still breathless. Still, he did not stop until he reached the frames where he and Eddy had been working.

With his heart pounding in panic he gathered his belongings together. He left the toolbox behind as he prepared to go. He thought of stopping at the security guard's booth, then decided against it. He wanted to be out of this terrible place and nothing else mattered.

Just as he turned to leave, the tenter frame switched itself on. The oven sprang to life, bellowing out its intense heat, and the chain began moving, slowly at first and then faster. Dave's heart leaped within his chest as he watched. He stared in horror as a new section of the chain emerged from the oven. It was coated with a thin, red film of blood.

Dave screamed in terror as Eddy's body appeared from the oven, attached to the chain. The body was baked by the intense heat of the oven; dried blood covered the mangled corpse. Dave's eyes were drawn to the left arm—the hand was missing.

Even as he turned and ran from the corpse he saw the security guard holding a bloody knife and smiling through twisted lips. Dave did not look back. He ran from the mill, clutching his belongings in one hand and his pipe in the other. He ran out the door and into the moonlight, passing the car without stopping. He crossed the parking lot and continued down the dirt road that led from the mill.

He saw a light in the distance. It shone from a house—part of the small mill town that surrounded this place. Once he was well away from the mill Dave paused and looked behind him. He stared in horror at the sight.

Every light in the place was turned on, every

machine was running—or so it sounded—and the huge tower-like chimney billowed smoke into the face of the full moon. The damn place had come to life!

Dave ran toward the house, leaving the terrible mill behind. When he reached the door he rapped loudly, shivering in the November breeze while he prayed for someone to answer. Finally, after what seemed like an eternity, the door opened ever so slightly.

"Who's there?" a man's voice asked suspiciously.

"Please. I need help," Dave panted. "I need a phone. Something terrible's happened."

The man opened the door a bit and studied Dave through the darkness.

"All right. Come on in. What's the matter, son?"

Dave noticed that the man held a pistol under his bathrobe.

"It's my partner. He's in the old mill. He's . . . he's dead."

"Dead? In the old mill? What the hell were you doing there?"

"We . . . we were filing a chain. They called us to fix a machine."

The man looked at Dave with questioning eyes.

"You sure you're all right? Did you fall or something?"

"No. I'm fine. It's my partner. . . ."

"Son," the man said quietly. "The old mill's closed. They haven't run that place in twelve, maybe thirteen years."

"Closed! What the hell do you mean? That's Dodgeville Dye! They called us to fix a chain!"

"No, son," he explained patiently, as if he were talking to a child. "Dodgeville Dye's down the road.

They built a new mill. They closed the old one some twelve years back. Condemned it when the security guard was killed there one night. They found him inside one of the ovens, his left hand missing, all cut up and burnt to a crisp. I'm sorry son. I guess I'll have to call the sheriff."

Dave walked to the window and looked out, back toward the old mill. It was completely deserted as if it *had* been closed for years.

He turned and faced the man once again. He held the pistol level and Dave dared not move again.

"Yeah, I guess you will," he said, as he slowly sat down on the floor and stared at his bloodstained shirt and pipe.

There Are No Ghosts In Catholic Spain
By Ray Bradbury

There Are No Ghosts In Catholic Spain

by Ray Bradbury

There are no ghosts in catholic Spain.
What, none?
None! Nil!
It goes uphill against the grain of their religion.
In any region you might go
The rain in Spain falls on a ghostless plain.
On juants about Castille you'll find it so:
No spirits, languished souls, dire haunts.
Those castles, ruined empty-jawwed, where gaunts
In England's guilt-prone nights might grow,
In Spain are only filled with cat-footfalls of rain.
The Papal architects have planned them out.
No ghosts are manufactured to weep here
From the start of a doleful month
To the end of a suffering year
The dead, the good/bad Church's dead?

(Learn it well!)
Jump straight to Heaven! Bang!
Or
Go to Hell!

No Loitering. says Mother Church. No hanging about
    the porch.
Up you go: Angel's wings!
Down you go: Torch!
No ectoplasm smoking the mirrored halls, pausing to
    admire
Its skull-face in the glass—mourning itself: "Alas!"
Up you jump—cherub's choir!
Down you go: fire! Not here: O, Lazarus, come forth!
Frights? are a thing blown North
On unfriendly winds to suffer all their bones in colder
    climes
Westminster's chimes do beckon them
Just so the English, dumb Protestants, can boast
That every high Lord's dried-up moat once drowned a
    skeleton
Or finds at midnight breakfasts a disturbed
And most distempered ghost.
Gah! let the fools maunder, let their most discourteous
Ghastlies wander, at loss for a sleep, raking and
Scratching the rats awash and awake in the wainscot.
Making the old mouldy flesh of lost Britain cold-creep
Much doubting of Heaven, uncertain of Flames,
Let Hamlet's Father's bones, cold Yorick's skull,
Fall down dumb stairs in dumber games—
And what the gain?
Better the Catholic hush and peace of soundless rain
That falls in Spain upon a ghostless plain . . .

Where God-tossed winds wash the innocent belfrey,
   whose bell
Sends all good souls crack-bang! high to Heaven!
And the bad?
Go to Hell!

Homecoming
By Frank Belknap Long

It's best to let the dead past . . . stay dead.

Homecoming
by Frank Belknap Long

"There's someone here to see you, Sir," Timothy Hargrave's elderly housekeeper said, pausing for an instant to glance backwards, as if to make sure that the creak from an ancient floorboard had not been made by an impatient visitor following her into the room.

It was a stately house, but old, *old* and that fact alone seemed to make Mrs. Lane more cautious than she might have been otherwise. It may have been caution also, or just her prim New England heritage that made her keep her voice low-keyed and accompanied by no more than the thinnest of smiles as she went on quickly: "I'm afraid he's a rather strange sort, Sir. What you would call—well, something of a *character.*"

The black leather armchair in which Hargrave was

sitting creaked a little as he swung about from the harbor-framing window through which he had been staring, although the chair was the opposite of ancient. There was an unblemished newness about it and a sliver of excelsior was still wedged in the footrest from the crate in which it had arrived three days previously.

"Sky overcast, threat of rain," Hargrave said, with the dull intonation of a TV weather announcer who has given up on a New England autumn. "Frankly, Mrs. Lane, it has been such a gloomy, dispiriting morning I'd welcome the visit of almost anyone. He must have some good reason for calling."

"It's all right then if I show him right in? He's waiting downstairs.

"Of course. Just one thing more, though. Is he a native or an outsider? From the way you speak of him—"

"I never set eyes on him before," Mrs. Lane said. "He must have walked from the bus stop or come in from the hills. Hill people sometimes stay out of sight for months or years, then just come walking in with a cup out for charity."

"It figures," Hargrave said. "In a town as small as East Elmsford you couldn't possibly mistake a native for an outsider, or vice versa. It's getting so every household pet—yes, even the seagulls—strike me as old acquaintances. Their individuality make them so instantly recognizable there's nothing left to get excited about."

"Your Uncle sometimes talked that way," Mrs. Lane said. "I never could see it, I'm afraid. It's people you know and meet every day I get most excited about."

"Because you never really know what they will say or do? Is that it?"

Miss Lane nodded.

"Well," Hargrave conceded. "You could be right. But that doesn't mean I'm wrong. Opposite sides of the same coin—that sort of thing. I just happen to find total strangers more of a challenge."

Looking a little flustered, as if she had been worsted in an argument she regretted having started, Mrs. Lane summoned another thin smile to her aid, and hurried from the room, shutting the door firmly behind her.

Hargrave remained for a moment motionless, listening to her footsteps receding down a long hallway and a double flight of stairs the opposite of rickety and yet, in some strange way, conveying that impression through some architectural peculiarity that seemed to amplify sound. Then he straightened and looked around him with the slight feeling of incredulity he could still not quite overcome whenever he allowed himself to dwell, however briefly, on the objects about him and the good fortune that had enabled him to possess them by right of inheritance.

The book-lined study walls, the late Victorian furnishings, and the small bronze bust of an earlier-period ancestor that stared down at him from a high embrasure directly overhead seemed no more incredible to him than the simple fact that he was back where he had wanted to be, for as long as he could remember.

The home of his uncle, the ancient, harbor-bordering dwelling, with its ivy-hung eaves and small-paned windows had seemed almost to float into his

111

possession with the rising of the tides when he had arrived from New York to occupy it. There had been an exchange of letters, of course, and papers to sign, and brief talks with the family lawyer immediately following his arrival.

Although legal documentation could sometimes turn estate-settling into a nightmare the still whip-sharp mind of the aging Jonathan Cage, in his neat solicitor's office on Somerset Street—uncluttered by the labors of fifty years—had achieved a miracle of simplification, and cut every item of red tape attached to the deed transfer in a matter of hours.

It all seemed remote to Hargrave now, remote and unimportant, although he had descended from the bus to become a new East Elmsford resident less than three weeks previously. There was only one thing of supreme importance. The house from which he had been taken in his infancy by his parents he now owned and unless some vicious maurader shot or strangled him in the night, wrapped his body in a sack, and lowered it into the harbor from a boat his tenancy would remain as secure as the rocks upon which the stately dwelling had been built.

Even the venerable Mrs. Lane had returned to serve him, as if she had known that he would someday have need for her, and had remained in the village in the unenviable isolation of a lonely widow. Her plight had been made unusually lonely by the pain that came from remembering that she had once been more than just pretty and had been courted for her looks alone. Faithful servants were rare and Mrs. Lane's devotion was a tribute indeed. He must remember, he told himself, to avoid upsetting her even slightly, as he had seemingly just done.

There was something else he had often tried to forget but it no longer seemed wise to blot it entirely from his mind. A frightening childhood memory could become worse through repression, or, at the very least, an attempt to repress it. He was certainly secure enough now in his heritage to bring it more frequently out into the open and contemplate it with sobriety and common sense.

Hargrave shut his eyes for a moment, thinking back; knowing that when Mrs. Lane tapped again at the door, he could dispel whatever remembered images from the remote past came flooding into his mind with a simple effort of will.

He had been little more than an infant in arms when his parents had quarreled with Uncle Charles, and left the house forever. Had he been four? Five even?

It didn't really matter. A child that age is like a little adult in some ways, with everything he sees and hears new to his experience and as fresh as a glistening dewdrop on the petals of a rose, or lilly pads on a crystal clear pond. Everything new and bright and strange comes in a rush and wisdom is forced on the untutored mind of a very young child by the sheer novelty of such an awakening.

Everything dark and terrible as well? Fearful things out of the past probably came less often to haunt the dreams of a child than the bright things. But come they often did, and the so-called "night fears" of childhood, as Hargrave had never needed to remind himself, had been a reality to him until he had passed the age of nine.

But it was not a night fear he was remembering now. It had taken place in broad daylight on the far side of the waterfall that thundered into white foam a quarter mile to the west of the house, and his toddler's feet had been firmly planted on a sloping, moss-covered rock so close to the onrushing water that if he had slipped and fallen drowning would have been his lot.

Terrible, accusing had been the faces of the three hill people who had emerged from the bullrushes on the opposite side of the stream and crossed to where he was standing on a bridge of flat rocks set almost end to end. They had stood for a moment shaking with rage and pointing toward the house, as if they were blaming him for something he could not possibly have done.

If his life had a century longer to last Hargrave was sure he would never forget how the three had looked in the eyes of the child he had once been. One was a woman well on in years with sunken cheeks and cavernous dark eyes, who hobbled when she moved, her left arm dangling lifelessly at her side. The second, who stood nearest to him, was a man of middle years, with even more cavernous eyes and a face so crisscrossed with deeply grooved wrinkles it seemed both mummylike and as old as Time.

The third was a youth of not more than eighteen or twenty, who held himself proudly erect, but in so tremulous a way he seemed about to fall forward on his face, or backwards into the stream.

It was the woman who moved swiftly past the two men to reach out and grab hold of him, despite her trembling. He could still feel the bite of her bony, snaking fingers, biting into the pudgy flesh of his wrist. And the words she had spoken still echoed in his mind as fearfully as they had on that long ago morning when something rebellious in the mind of a child still dangerously close to babyhood had made him go roaming.

"Charles Hargrave must be made to stop! Do you hear, child. He is slowly killing us all."

The older man had laughed then, in a harsh and mocking way. "I have always known you were a fool, Miranda. Now I am sure of it. To say such things to a wee one, barely old enough to totter."

He had broken free then, by wrenching, tearing at the distraught woman's tightening fingers, until she cried out in pain. Babyish hands or not, they had somehow succeeded in freeing him, and he had fled, stumbling and crying, back to the house, his little more than swaddling clothes ripped by brambles and prickly thorns. It was possible, of course, and he had given much thought to it, that was the woman had simply released him, and the cry he had mistaken for physical pain had been one of inner torment.

"The gentleman is here, sir," Mrs. Lane called through the door she had closed behind her three or four minutes previously out of respect for his privacy—a privacy he had himself violated by letting himself be visited by phantoms from the past. But he had faced something again under changed circumstances that had convinced him that he had everything to gain by stopping, once and for all, his previous flights *from* the past.

By bringing it all out into the open again he had done himself no harm and actually felt better for it. It was what every pyscho-therapist could have told him, he realized, but he had never consulted one and had no intention of doing so. In the most pleasant fantasy that had ever come to him he had pictured himself offering Freud a good cigar, patting him on the back, and assuring him that no one would judge him too harshly for his rigidly old-fashioned ideas about sex when he had accomplished so much in other directions. And Freud, looking grateful, had confessed that what he most dreaded was to be thought a fuddy-duddy. 'Just between ourselves, you know, I'm not really like that at all.'

He suddenly realized that the door had opened and closed and the visitor was in the room. On failing to get an instant reply to her announcement Mrs. Lane had apparently taken it upon herself to admit the man anyway. That did not anger or surprise Hargrave, for it was surely her right to be strong-willed about something for which he was entirely to blame.

It was just that he had been carried away for a moment by the phantoms from the past, and justifying all of that to himself had made the arrival of his visitor seem a great deal less important.

He was facing the window again and he took his time in turning, just why he could not have said. Perhaps it was because at such a moment even the creak of the easy chair he preferred to postpone until he had regained complete mastery of himself. There was only a slight shuffling sound by the door to make him aware that he was no longer alone.

It was hard for him to believe the instant he had swung completely about that Mrs. Lane had not done the tall, big-boned and heavily tanned man who stood

116

just inside the doorway an injustice in referring to him as a character. There was nothing in the least eccentric about his aspect, from his rough-hewn lumberjack's face to his tan windbreaker jacket, and calm outward manner. There was unmistakable poise and dignity even in the way he held himself, standing very straight and still with his level gray eyes mirroring the kind of firm determination that commands instant respect.

Was it some eccentricity of behavior then, something he had said or done on his arrival that had placed him, in Mrs. Lane's eyes, distinctly beyond the pale, from a well-bred New Englander's point of view? There could be no doubt she was difficult to please in that respect, but it hardly seemed likely that she would have described him as "a rather strange sort" if something about him had not jarred on her sensibilities as soon as they had exchanged a few words.

Hargrave knew he should have been the first to speak, if only to put a visitor he had agreed to see and who had every right to be standing there completely at his ease. But so simple an act of courtesy seemed less important to him than satisfying his curiosity as to what the other might say if he remained silent.

It proved the shrewdest decision he could possibly have made. The instant the man began to speak everything that Mrs. Lane had said about him stood explained. His calmness vanished and his words were so abrupt, so without preamble, it seemed as if some smouldering grievance that had been gnawing at him for months or years had suddenly erupted in an uncontrollable burst of rage.

"Charles Hargrave had only one purpose in mind

when he made you his heir. There was no one else he could have bequeathed this property to with any assurance that his work would be carried on. You were born in this house, you are a Hargrave and you are a man of high intelligence. Capable of great loyalty too, I have no doubt. You would respect the provisions of your uncle's will."

For a moment Hargrave could only stare. He had not anticipated such an outburst, or knew how to contend with it. The man had paid him a compliment, in a way, despite his rage. And he, too, seemed to be possessed of a fairly high degree of intelligence, or he could not have spoken as he had.

"I'm completely in the dark concerning all of this," Hargrave heard himself saying, knowing that he lied, but feeling it would be unwise to do otherwise.

"I can't believe you do not know," the big man raged on, with no trace of moderation in his voice. "Surely you are aware of what the residents of East Elmsford think about the 'hill people.' It is their term, not ours. It suggests primitiveness, backwardness, as if we came from an ancestral stock that very little can be done to salvage."

"I have never thought that," Hargrave heard himself protesting. "Or said it."

"No? Then how do you regard them? With pity perhaps? Between pity and contempt there is the thinnest of dividing lines. The instant you start pitying someone you begin to feel superior."

Whether or not the statement was a perceptive one would have given Hargrave no concern at that particular moment if something in the other's eyes had not convinced him that he was taking it with a dangerous degree of seriousness. To discuss what was less than admirable in human nature in general terms was one thing. To make a personal issue of it quite another.

"I've always tried to avoid the kind of pity you have in mind," Hargrave said quickly. "Real compassion comes only through understanding and it is devoid of the self-complacency that can enable a man to feel in any way superior."

"It is very easy to talk that way," his visitor countered, seemingly not in the least mollified. "I urge that you listen carefully to what I've come to tell you, instead of making excuses for the kind of mistake Charles Hargrave made and you will make also—if you choose to ignore my warning."

The big man paused for an instant, but went on too quickly for Hargrave to say anything in reply. "Sixty or seventy years ago, all over America, there were many small, isolated groups of people living in extreme poverty, particularly in densely forested regions, it was a great mistake to think of as primitive or backward. Their numbers have been dwindling fast, and today it is only rarely that a man or woman can descend from a bus in a town like East Elmsford, explore such regions and encounter more than one or two of them in a day of searching.

"But they are there. Make no mistake about it. Year by year they are growing in inner strength and wisdom, and what they have always sought—and they were not primitive to begin with—is another kind of reality in which there is no past, present or future. There is a plane of existence where time as we know it has no meaning. It is a world of NOW. It is always changing and yet it is always the same, for what happens there doubles back upon itself and becomes what it was before."

"I am familiar with such occult or semi-mystical speculation." Hargrave heard himself saying. "The entire structure of Eastern thought rests upon it, in varying degrees, and it has been embraced by the young so widely today that I would be a fool to disclaim all interests in it. But taking it seriously as providing a few possible clues as to the nature of ultimate reality—about which we can know nothing—and actually believing it are two quite different things."

"Charles Hargrave took it seriously, as I think you know," the big man said. "There are several disciplines that can enable a man of high intelligence and singleness of purpose to enter that world. But to attempt to do so alone and to fathom its mysteries unaided would be so dangerous an undertaking that it could end with his destruction. He must have the support and draw upon the strength and wisdom of others who have long practiced such disciplines."

"And those others?"

"I think you know who they were. I think you know also that my people did not provide him with the key willingly. They fought against being drained, used, in that way. But they were unable to defend themselves against a man like Charles Hargrave, who could communicate with them without warning, and take possession of their minds before they could awaken to the horror of what was happening to them.

"Do you understand? He attacked their minds like some sharp-fanged Dracula of that timeless world,

120

crippling them physically as well and forcing them to protect him with their guidance and wisdom, to make his own journey less dangerous.

"My people gained their knowledge slowly and cautiously, step by patient step across the years. He snatched it from them far too quickly, at the cost of shattered lives."

Hargrave's visitor seemed to draw himself up, although he had been standing very straight and to become even taller than he had been.

"You have come here to reclaim your heritage, as you have every right to do. You are young and proud and headstrong and I would be a fool indeed if I failed to understand what errors youth can commit in a careless way without considering the cost. But I warn you—continue with Charles Hargrave's research—he called it that in his blind folly—and you will be stopped, as he was stopped. I and my people have now found a way to fight fire with fire."

Hargrave's visitor turned abruptly, as if satisfied that the message he had come to deliver had fallen on fertile soil and there was nothing to be gained by pursuing it further. Before Hargrave could say a word in reply to the man's final threat—there could be no question as to its nature—he had crossed the room and was at the door. But he turned just once before wrenching it open and passing out into the hall.

Without withdrawing his gaze from Hargrave's face he raised his hand to his own face and did something to it. It happened so quickly that Hargrave could not be sure. But it was as if the man had stripped away a thin gauzelike mask that concealed something about his features that had not been visible before. They looked very much the same, and yet—it was more than just a change of expression.

It has been said that there are bruisings inflicted on the mind that can contort human features in a permanent and unmistakable way. It was the results of such a bruising that Hargrave seemed to be looking at now, a bruising such as the medieval torture victims must have known.

Then the door opened and closed and the Hargrave's visitor was gone.

Hargrave sat very still, firmly telling himself two things. It was very unlikely that the man had removed anything from his face at all, or that it had been altered in any way. The confrontation he had just endured with as much patience as he could manage would have upset almost anyone's nerves enough to make him imagine that a slight change in the light as it slanted down over a face had brought about a much greater change.

The second thing that made him feel that he had allowed himself to become unnecessarily agitated by what his visitor had said was the simple fact that it followed a well-known pattern. In both life and literature there was hardly a figure more instantly recognizable than the one his visitor had presented—a man born amidst squalor, in deprived circumstances, acquiring at college or through self-education the kind of knowledge that enabled him to speak with a semblance of authority, before returning to his people to champion their cause.

It did not matter that the cause might not be worth championing despite all of his claims to the contrary. Or that, while worthy, it could load to the kind of false accusations that had been leveled against the house's previous occupant, or, for that matter, the present one, who might have been almost anyone, but happened to be Charles Hargrave's nephew.

What had probably mattered most to his visitor, Hargrave told himself, was the man's feeling of self-importance and the care he'd taken to keep from diminishing it by making all kinds of exaggerated charges in the most aggressive possible fashion.

Such people were bullies at heart, whether they realized it or not.

Hargrave was almost sure that he heard, drifting up through the house with the strange way it had of seeming to amplify sound, the voice of Mrs. Lane ushering his visitor out. But he waited to be sure, continuing to sit motionless until he heard the unmistakable sound of the front door slamming shut and causing the faintest of vibrations to pass through the room.

Hargrave was not the kind of man it was safe for anyone to attack verbally, even if one or two back-handed compliments had accompanied such an attack—particularly if he was being held accountable for something he had not yet done and might decide never to do.

He waited for a moment longer, to make absolutely sure that he had regained all of his shattered composure.

Then he got up, crossed the study to the wall safe he had fallen into the habit of keeping locked, although a visit from a burglar in East Elmsford seemed unlikely, opened it with three quick dial adjustments, and took out Charles Hargrave's letter. He also removed a bulky manuscript with its pages held together by a large paperclip. The letter and manuscript had arrived in a flat parcel with a smudged and indistinguishable postmark, which he had discarded. Mrs. Lane had brought the parcel up to him and he had immediately assumed that the postman must have delivered it, since Mrs. Lane had said nothing to contradict that assumption, and he had heard departing footsteps. It had also been the right time in the morning for mail to be delivered.

Returning to his chair by the window he reseated himself, and read the letter for the third time, leaning forward a little to overcome the poor light which filtered down outside through the gray overcast. The shrill cry of a gull wheeling and dipping in the harbor came to his ears at precisely that moment, but he refused to consider it as any kind of omen.

"My dear nephew," the letter began and it almost seemed as if his uncle had walked into the room, and was standing at his side, with the strong, firm hand remembered from childhood tightening on his shoulder as he talked on.

Hargrave shut his eyes, as he had done once before in an effort to recover some small part of the past that was important to him. The letter had clearly been written before his uncle's death and so delayed in transit that it had arrived only a fortnight ago. And Mrs. Lane, when questioned later, hadn't been quite sure whether the parcel had been delivered by the mailman, or simply left by the front door by person, or persons unknown.

"You should have asked me right away," he could remember her saying. "Now I can't be sure. I brought the entire package right up to you, as you'll recall."

It had done him no good to remind her that he had heard the bell ring and what sounded like the postman departing on his usual morning round. How could she have become so uncertain about an occurrence less than two weeks old? A faulty memory was the last thing he would have associated with her, and a parcel that important—Of course his uncle's name hadn't been on it, and she had brought him several other small parcels since his arrival and two or three of them, containing mail order items sent by express, hadn't been handed to her by the postman.

Still, it was all very strange. What made it even stranger—the postman couldn't remember delivering it either and since it hadn't been insured the post office had no record of it.

The strangeness went beyond even that. When he'd opened the parcel why had he kept its contents a secret from Mrs. Lane? Why hadn't he discussed it with her immediately and asked her exactly how it had arrived? Its delayed arrival had angered him, and it was the sort of thing he ordinarily would have discussed with her, even if he hadn't gone so far as to read the letter to her, from beginning to end.

He was not actually re-reading it now. He was keeping his eyes closed and letting a remembered voice that seemed as real to him as the pressure of his uncle's firm hand do that for him.

"My illness has been diagnosed as fatal. I may have a few weeks left, or I could go tomorrow. One thing only dominates all of my thinking now. I have enclosed some instructions that will enable you to pass, with just a little study, into the trancelike state it has

125

taken me years to master.

"I am pinning all of my hopes on this: That a man of great intellectual curiosity, such as you have now become, will not draw back from exploring the unknown when he sits in my study, in the house I have just bequeathed to him, in a will that no one will be able to challenge. Yes, my dear nephew, you are fated to become my heir, for good or ill.

"I am writing this at a great distance from East Hampton, and I doubt if I shall live to return. Why I took so long a journey at this time, and its precise nature are matters of importance to me alone. All I ask is that you think of me at times and remember me with kindness and the walks we took together long ago, with the thunder of the waterfall loud in our ears. You were a toddler indeed and even at that time I had need of a cane."

Hargrave opened his eyes then, and brought his gaze to bear on the neatly typed lines of the letter in his hand. The voice from the past was gone, as if the closing paragraphs were of so precise and instructional a nature that his uncle would have wished him to remove his eyes from the page. There was a point or two which might otherwise have been missed, even though he had read the letter before.

There was one point that had been made unmistakably clear. The trance state into which he would pass if he followed the even more detailed instructions in the manuscript that he had placed beneath the letter before bringing it closer to the light would be of brief duration. It was a way of penetrating the unknown that could be repeated again and again, in the days and weeks ahead, until he had acquired so great a knowledge of the timeless world Charles Hargrave had explored through years of patient research that he might never wish to return. The more shiningly real it became—

For the barest instant Hargrave shut his eyes again and a line from Tennyson came into his mind. "To follow knowledge like a sinking star, beyond the utmost bounds of human thought."

Almost, it seemed, without actually willing to do so, he put the letter aside and removed the paperclip from the bulky manuscript.

Hargrave was still sitting in the easy chair, slumped a little forward and utterly still when Mrs. Lane came into the room four hours later to announce that supper was ready and waiting on the table.

For a moment his stillness seemed to alarm her, and she took firm hold of his shoulders and shook him. Then, as if ashamed of her boldness she stepped quickly back, for what could be more indecorous for a housekeeper than the taking of such a liberty when she had no way of knowing if her concern was justified.

Hargrave's face had a rigidly set, almost masklike look and only his jaw hung slack. It was not an unusual look for a man so overcome by drowsiness that he had fallen into a deep sleep from which he could not be easily aroused. But such an aspect could also be the most telling indication of a sudden and fatal heart attack.

That such a possibility had occurred to Miss Lane was evident from her distraught expression when she began shaking him again, more violently this time and with all of her scruples forgotten.

His body swayed a little with her tugging, back and

forth in the chair. But he slumped even lower, like a corpse that had been made to seem animated in a wholly artificial way. She seemed aware of that, for her right hand left his shoulder and darted quickly to his arm in what was clearly an effort to keep his body in balance.

She gripped his arm tightly and even tried to raise it, but gave up trying when something about it—a leaden heaviness perhaps—sharply increased her alarm. She could neither raise nor lower it, or bend it at the elbow and the futility of what she was attempting to do seemed to strike her suddenly with the force of a physical blow.

She leapt back and away from the chair with a look of despairing horror in her eyes. And it was at that precise moment that Timothy Hargrave spoke.

"The region through which I am passing is becoming more and more strange."

His voice was tremulous and scarcely rose above a whisper and in some hard-to-define way was like that of a man under some irresistible compulsion to speak his thoughts aloud to someone—anyone at all—who might be listening or just to himself alone.

"It's as if—I were inside a vast beehive with glimmering many-tiered honeycombs suspended in the darkness and lighting it up in all directions. Underfoot it is like a desert waste, but my feet sink into some soft, spongy substance that is quite unlike sand. There are gray rocks scattered about but no plants or animals of visible size. When I strain my ears I can hear faint rustlings and scurrying sounds, but beyond that—nothing. Not even a sighing of the wind."

For a moment his voice seemed to lose its tremor, as

if some ingrained habit of speaking with scholarly accuracy was asserting itself, despite his fear, despite everything. Just the importance of being a careful observer, to justify the most terrible of risks, had seemingly taken, however briefly, complete possession of his thoughts.

His breathing suddenly quickened, forcing him to pause when he spoke again his brief calmness was gone. There was a rising excitement in his voice, but though it became tremulous again it seemed less heavily laden with fear.

"I am no longer alone. Three of the hill people are walking at my side. They are lame and faltering, but they are helping me to go on. Not physically. They are providing no support of that kind. But they are enabling me to understand better the meaning and importance of everything that Uncle Charles accomplished. I know that they hate me. I can see it in their eyes. The demands I am making on them for support and guidance are causing them pain. They would turn on me if they could, but their will to resist has been broken now. Uncle has seen to that."

For a moment there was silence again in the room. Then Hargrave shifted about in his chair and raised himself until he was sitting almost straight.

"Everything about me is changing again. But the hill people are still at my side. It is as if some invisible force is drawing us onward toward a vast, brightly lighted cone of impossible dimensions, its colors flickering, changing while—"

There was another pause and then Hargrave cried out because of something he had seen. What that something was Miss Lane seemed not to care, for she

129

had summoned the strength of will at last to emerge from the far corner of the study to which she had retreated when Hargrave had first begun to speak and to fling herself down at his side. She clutched frantically at his wrist, with a look of desperate pleading in her eyes.

"It was like that with your Uncle," she cried. "The hill people helped him too. But never enough—oh, never enough. You can still turn back, as he could not do the last time he went into the timeless world. You must try, before it is too late. You must—"

"Mrs. Lane! Mrs. Lane! Where are you?" Hargrave almost screamed the words. "I can hear you, but I cannot see you at all. The visitor is here again. I heard him descending the stairs, I heard the front door slam. I thought he had gone. But he is here again, right in my path. He is stretching out his hand straight toward me. But not in friendship or forgiveness. He is condemning me for what I have done and his face—it is even more ravaged than I had thought. He has suffered more than the others and his eyes—"

"You can still come back!" Mrs. Lane pleaded, her voice rising even more. "It is your first journey. There may still be time for you to save yourself."

"No, it is too late! He is saying hideous things to me. He is repeating what he said before, but now the others are repeating it too. He is saying they have found a way to stop me, as uncle was stopped. And something bright, blinding, is darting from his hand."

The flickering began in a far corner of the study, where Mrs. Lane had been crouching and far from where they now were. Hargrave had begun to shake, like a man in the grip of an instantaneous palsy, and

Mrs. Lane's ancient countenance had become so white that it seemed like the face of a waxen doll.

She did not speak or move again, just sat staring at the flickering beside Hargrave's chair until it turned into a sheet of flame that climbed both of the walls and swept toward the window and the easy chair and of course herself. She seemed to feel that she could do nothing more to save the man in the chair and vanished just before the flames reached out toward her, as if a fierce current of air had swept in from the window and carried her off across the russet and gold New England countryside to a cemetery that was peaceful and quiet, where she had reposed for ten years.

Hargrave was not so mercifully spared, and the flames swept in upon him with a brightness that outshone the sun at midday, when there was no gray overcast to dim its rays. Then he, too, was gone, but his shrieks continued to echo throughout the house for a moment, from crisscrossing oak rafters upstairs and down until they died away into silence, amidst the continuous roar of the flames.

Sheriff John Brigley turned from the dispersing crowd and made his way to the car of aging Jonathan Cage, who had come to see what the commotion had been all about. Despite his seventy-eight years Cage remained a man of sprightly mien, with dark hair only slightly sprinkled with gray and the perennial curiosity of a much younger man.

"I was puzzled by what seems to be happening here," Cage explained, when the sheriff had frowned and wiped his brow, after removing his wide-brimmed hat as a gesture of respect for a man he had admired for thirty years.

"The glow drew quite a crowd," Brigley said. "I can't explain it. I doubt if any one can. But for several hours, beginning at about six o'clock, it almost seemed as if Charles Hargrave's house had burned to the ground for the second time, after ten years."

"But there was no fire here last night," Cage protested. "There couldn't have been."

"Naturally not. You were Hargrave's solicitor, so you ought to know better than anyone else. There was no fire here, period. But there was a distinct glow, apparently, for several hours. It must have been caused by some unusual kind of electrical phenomenon."

"Well, it was nobody's loss," Cage said, with a sigh. "I mean, when the house actually went, and drew a much larger crowd. Charles only living heir didn't live long enough to hear the will read, as you know. I wrote him a long letter but when it arrived he was in a New York hospital with double pneumonia. He lived just three days after that.

"From what I've heard Timothy Hargrave was a young man who would have gone far," the sheriff said. "A Madison Avenue executive at twenty-seven or so."

"That's right," Cage said. "Possibly he wouldn't have cared to live permanently in a sleepy New England town. One never knows, though. It was a beautiful house, despite its age, and he would have inherited enough money to live on for life, despite *his* age. He lived here with his parents until he was five, and there are childhood memories that can act as a magnet."

"I've something here I may as well show you,"

Brigley said. "Sand spirals can take unusual forms, and the same electrical phenomenon that produced the glow could have blown considerable sand in from the beach and swirled it about right where Hargrave's house once stood. A strong wind could do that, too, but there was no wind last night. The Edward's kid, as you know, is a camera fiend and he has a Polaroid—a quite expensive one. Well, about an hour ago, before the ground became trampled, and I arrived he took this photograph."

The sheriff handed Cage the photograph and nodded. "Sort of odd though, isn't it? A dust spiral shaped like a tall, muscular man who could be young or old, but somehow conveys an impression of youth. *With one hand thrown before his face*. Cringing back a bit too, as if he didn't like what he saw coming at him. And in the photograph the ground all around the spiral has a blackened, charred look. Ground's been trampled since, as I said, and it doesn't look that way now. Nothing there now but shoe prints."

"I see," Cage said. "Well—thank you."

He handed the photograph back and leaned forward to start his car motor humming.

The sheriff accepted the hint in good grace and stepped back.

"See you around, Sheriff," Cage said.

Compliments of
The Season
By John Brizzolara

Not only good things come in small packages . . .

Compliments of the Season

by John Brizzolara

The doorbell rang. Frank Darby: fortyish, fresh from the shower late on a Friday afternoon, his hangover banished, answered it. He turned down the volume on the stereo from which bland, Muzak versions of Christmas carols issued from WPAT. He set a fresh scotch next to the Christmas cards he had just received and his black Cartier address book. He hadn't sent any cards this year himself but he intended to make a note of the people who had sent one to him. Sound business; it paid to know who your friends were. He crossed the white shag carpet to the buzzer/intercom and pressed the "Talk" button. "Yes, Harry." He said curtly to the doorman.

"Package for you, Mr. Darby. Messenger."

"Okay, Harry. Bring it up for me will you if it's not too big?"

"Sure, Mr. Darby. It's small, real small."

"Well good things come in small packages." He said automatically.

"Yes sir."

He took his finger off the intercom and walked distractedly back to the desk. Packages had been coming with regularity for weeks. Baskets of fruit, cheeses and wines, out of print 78 LP's, objets d'art, cases of liquor and liquers all from account executives wooing him like sappy school boys. They wanted his account. Still, it was nice to think of them as friends and for a moment he allowed himself that little indulgence. He ran through a mental checklist, matching names with holiday payola and he grew puzzled. He thought of the package on it's way up on the elevator and could not, for the life of him imagine who might have sent it.

The news was on the radio. The newscaster sounded bored, nearly sedated as he spoke of The Long Island Railroad strike, the breaking of diplomatic relations with some country in the middle east and The Soho Strangler. 'Stupid.' Frank thought to himself. 'Why The Soho Strangler? Most of the victims hadn't even been strangled and only one was found in Soho. Typical media bullshit. Creeping New York Postism. Sensationalism was a disease with news people.' In sleepy tones the voice on WPAT informed his listeners. ". . . and fourth victim identified as Louise Maynard, controversial talk show hostess of NBC TV's New Dawn. She was found at 6:45 this morning in front of the side entrance to The Lunar Light Occult Bookstore on E. 53rd street by Oliver Ware, the proprietor of the bookshop and resident of the building. Pronounced dead on arrival from multiple stab wounds, Ms. Maynard was identified at Lenox Hill hospital by. . . ."

Frank snapped off the radio. Who wanted to hear such grisly things at this time of the year? They should concentrate on more seasonal, upbeat news items. 'That's what I'd do!' He told himself smugly, 'If I were managing a news program. Too many stabbings and whatnot around Christmastime and they're bound to loose listeners. Why people will do just what I did. Tune out. You can't have Christmas carols one minute and the next some gruesome. . . .'

The doorchimes sounded and he remembered the package. "Coming, Harry." He called out and set down the drink he had been absently sipping at. He opened the door and took a small, rectangular box from the doorman. It was covered in plain brown paper with the words, FRANK DARBY 113 E. 83rd St. written on it with cramped but artistic handwriting. There was no return address. "Thank you, Harry." He said, frowning at the package.

"Yes, sir." The doorman made no motion to leave.

"Oh yes. Here, Harry." Frank produced a dollar bill from his money clip and gave it to the uniformed man. "Merry Christmas."

"Thanks, Mr. Darby." He said walking to the elevator, his finger poised to press the "Down" button. Frank did not notice the ironic tone in the man's voice. "I bet it's a watch." He offered as he saw Frank still standing in the doorway of the apartment turning the package over in his hands and looking vaguely uncomfortable.

"Could be." Frank said waving to Harry and closed

the door. He suddenly found himself hoping that that's what it was, just a watch, though he already owned several. He also had the inexplicable certainty that it was not, though the package looked to be about the right size. The thing was, he simply wasn't expecting anymore gifts. All his business associates had been accounted for, he had no family, very few people had his mailing address. His ex-wife would hardly send him a gift unless it was a bomb. . .but it certainly wasn't her handwriting. He put the package to his ear and tried smiling away the growing sense of disquiet he was experiencing. 'Maybe it is a watch.' He laughed hollowly to himself and listened for the tick. 'Or a bomb from Maurine.' There was only the sound of paper against his sideburns.

He stared across the room and into the picture window that overlooked the East River and Queens, though he didn't see the nocturnal cityscape. If he had, if he had seen the string of Christmas lights along Second Avenue, the red and green spotlights atop a luxury high-rise and the blinking MERRY CHRISTMAS HAPPY NEW YEAR in the window of a neighboring building he would have merely cracked his tired joke to himself about how this is the time of year the whole world turns into Puerto-ricans. Instead, he looked at his reflection in the plate glass. His reflection looked back at him, fidgeting with a small package. He saw a balding man in a three piece Cardin suit, a bit of a corporation up front which the pin-striped vest obscured snugly. The reflection had broad shoulders and a wide, manly stance. Not a bad figure of a self made man. Frank Darby of Darby Products Inc. There was no explanation for the tinge of fear he detected in the eyes looking back at him from the window. Was that a tremble he saw or did the wind rattle the pane glass ever so slightly? It must have been the wind for he did feel a chill.

He crossed quickly to the desk and took his glass, tossing back half of it at once and wishing it were brandy despite his bad heart. He was consciously wondering how much worse brandy could really be for your heart than scotch, and shuffling the address book and cards around on the desk when he suddenly thought: Sarah! That was it, it was from his secretary Sarah Krassner. Of course, he sighed a little with relief and it seemed to echo in the empty apartment. His fingers flew over the tightly stretched piece of twine and the Scotch-taped edges of the paper as if in a hurry to confirm this happy thought or to get something over with quickly. He hadn't received anything from Sarah and here it was the 23rd, he told himself. 'Why she probably ran right out after work realizing the date and then sent a messenger. . . .'

He nearly convinced himself and allayed the cold, baseless trepidation he could not understand.

When he had removed the plain wrapping he saw that there was another layer of paper, a black, parchment-like stuff. He remembered then that Sarah had given him black onyx book ends a week ago for his Christmas gift.

That he should be so suddenly and irrationally anxiety-ridden over an unexpected gift began now to annoy him. He tore away the black paper with quick, angry fingers as if unmasking an intruder caught in his home. The inner wrapping fell away to reveal a glossy, hand painted box. It was a bright red, the

141

color of new blood and bordered by tiny symbols around the edges of a kind which Frank Darby had never seen before. The box itself reminded him of those hand-painted Russian music boxes, candy dishes or cigarette containers which usually depicted a wintry scene: children skating or sleigh rides. This box had no such illustration on it, only the odd symbols like characters in some long forgotten alphabet.

He looked at it from all sides, searching for an inscription or clue to its origin. There was nothing. He put it beneath the harsh light of his goose-necked writing lamp. His heart sounded in his ears, a plodding maniacal bass drum. He asked himself again why this feeling of entrapment and repulsion but he could find no answer that made any sense. The box itself seemed to be the source of his nameless, gathering terror, a kind of dark battery running its charge of dread through his fingers, up through his arms and into some secret place in his mind or heart that knew what there was to fear.

With a quick, convulsive movement and an involuntary whimper he pried the lid off the enameled teakwood box. Inside was a piece of green silk. With fingers now like pale, trembling worms he loosened the silk. He let out a sharp laugh and mopped his forehead with a handkerchief when he saw what the box contained.

It was the feather of some undoubtedly rare bird. It was of a lush, scarlet color with a natural pattern of concentric circles in deepening shades of blue and silver, like moonlit ripples on a still lake. It was a thing of extraordinary beauty and he could not recall seeing a bird anywhere with plummage like this, even in the artistic renderings of the most fevered imaginations. He picked it up and saw that it was more than a feather. It was a quill, about ten inches long from its widest point to its tip made of finest gold.

His fear was momentarily forgotten as he allowed himself to admire the singular beauty of the thing. He could not guess who had sent it or from what strange creature it was fashioned from, but he was not a man on whom beauty and rarity were lost. His collection of pre-Columbian artifacts had been judged to be possibly the finest in New York. The paintings in his dining room were accrued with infinite patience and a relentless eye. He was never seen with a woman who could be considered less than breathtaking. He had married the most beautiful woman in the world in fact—that she had turned to other women for love in the end in no way marred her physical perfection. Yes, whoever had sent this thing to him knew him in an uncanny way, knew he would be seduced by its almost Platonic, otherworldly exquisitness. He no longer cared who had sent it. No doubt they would reveal themselves all too soon and what it was he could do for them. 'Oh, yes,' he chuckled. 'They'll make themselves known and I'll do for them whatever it is they want because I must have this thing.' He renewed his chuckle and thought, 'To Hell with them, I do have it!'

It was then that he noticed a tiny vial of red liquid beneath a fold in the green silk. It was a simple little glass bottle, the size of a perfume sample. It had a black stopper at its neck. He lifted it to the light and peered into it. It was nearly opaque but not quite, like very thin blood, the blood of a bird perhaps. "Why it's ink!" He said aloud smiling at the bizarre touch. He set the tiny bottle down and removed the stopper. He poised the quill over the stuff and daintily dipped the gold point into the liquid. Looking around for something to write on, he took one of the Christmas cards he had received and spread it face down on the desk. He formulated a simple phrase in his head; Season's Greetings, and set the pen to the white space.

The quill seemed to shiver and dart. It jumped lightly in his hand with a life of its own. Darby felt the returning sensation of icy alarm. He looked down at the paper, to what he/it had written and the deafening pulse sounded again in his ears. In bold, blood red letters, in a mockingly beautiful handwriting that was not his own, the pen had written, "Good evening Mister Darby. This night will see you in Hell."

At first Darby did not read the words. He stared with a mixture of apprehension and incredulity at the quill as if it were, after all, some sort of novelty toy, a dime store gag. And then he read the words. He wanted to drop the pen as if it were scalding him. He wanted to flee from the thing, run and never stop. But Frank Darby couldn't move. An invisible weight pressed him to the chair and the desk. Unseen bonds held his hand to the quill like a thousand gossamer threads of evil. He shut his eyes, it would go away. He was having an attack of some kind. He had been working very hard, the past eight weeks were the peak season. He had been pushing himself. The drinking too, he admitted looking at the scotch and thinking of his recently conquered hangover. 'Overdoing things a bit, that's all.'

He told himself these things with his eyes clamped

firmly shut, his breath coming in ragged gasps while his hand, like a puppet's, raised the quill, dipped the point into the tiny bottle and set it back onto the paper. While his hand shook, the pen did not.

"I know who you are, Mr. Darby." It wrote. "I know all about you. I have come for you. I have in the name of Linda Grant, Alicia Weldman, Maria DeCorona and Louise Maynard. I have come in the name of others Mr. Darby, others whose identity, names, like my own, you needn't concern yourself over. The methods by which I am communicating to you now involve certain arts, the very existence of which I'm sure you disbelieve and are unimportant for our purposes at the moment. It suffices for the moment that you possess me in your murderous fist, just as I (or shall I say we) have possessed you in the past and will more fully in the immediate future."

The quill flew across the page now and then stopping to jerk Darby's frozen hand to the inkwell.

"Down to business then, eh Mr. Darby? Let me illuminate things for you. Allow me to fill in the gaps of your recollection of your recent nightlife so you will see how it is you must come with me tonight. So that you will come gladly, with eyes open, to a place where you shall be surrounded by others like yourself. Others who understand, who sympathize, who know why you had to kill them all.

"Linda Grant was almost perfect wasn't she Frank? A wondrous, fragile creature except for one little thing: her laugh. Believe me Frank I know what you mean; to hear that brassy, sluttish laughter rising up through that delicate throat was too much for you to bear. You're very sensitive. You had to stop it didn't you? Do you remember now? Of course you do. You followed her to the door of her apartment building. She was still laughing at the dirty joke the man told her at the bar and you put your fingers around her neck and stopped it. It felt so good."

The pen stopped, poised over the inkwell and fluttered, perhaps from a slight draft—but Frank sensed it was laughing.

"And Alicia Weldman. Too much make-up. That was it, wasn't it Frank? Oh I agree, I agree. She didn't need all that lipstick and grease and powder. She would have been perfect except for all that filthy paint. So you showed her didn't you? You showed her with soap and water in the ladies room at the theatre. And when she screamed you held her head in the sink under the water, the hot, cleansing water until all the make-up came off and she was dead.

"You see, Mr. Darby? I know. I understand."

Frank read the words trailing from the point of the quill. The neat, ornate handwriting had filled two sides of a Christmas card. Frank dutifully, helplessly provided another for it. As he read, he remembered. It came back to him in a flood of loathing and disgust and desperate denial. Yet he did remember and the thing, the pen, whatever its intentions or motivations, whoever had sent it that spelled it all out for him, seemed to genuinely understand.

"Maria was a pig wasn't she Frank? And she could have been so regal, so devastatingly mysterious and exotic with those bituminous, fiery eyes, those sculpted cheekbones, her impeccable bearing. Yet you watched her day after day in that restaurant on Third Avenue stuffing her face, buying candy bars at the

146

newsstand downstairs in The Darby Building. Eating, always eating: donuts and junk food. Greasy, sticky, fatty things. Everytime you passed her desk she would be chewing like a cow. You watched her get fat. Well, almost fat eh, Frank? You saved her from that. She'll never be fat now. You got her address and waited for her in the delicatessen that night. You knew she'd come and she did. She bought a Sarah Lee cheesecake and you went out behind her. Then, in that vacant lot, with a knife at her throat, you taught her a lesson. You made her eat all of it right there for you. Then, — and I like this touch Frank — you made her eat a brick. You brought it down again and again into her face and mouth until her head became much like the jelly filling in the donuts she was so fond of. You showed her. The little pig."

Frank fought for control of his other hand. He tried to bring the glass of scotch to his lips. His hand shook. The ice rattled and he dropped it to the carpet. Oh God, he remembered all of it. The nightmares, the blackouts, the drinking to forget and the forgetting because he was drunk. It all washed over him now; the faces of the women in life and in death, the crystalline, icy logic that led him to the acts, the unholy exhileration, the shame of the sticky dampness in his pants and the euphoric righteousness he felt just before he would forget everything.

His right hand continued to jerk puppet-like across the third Christmas card. With his left hand he brought the entire bottle of scotch to his white lips.

"Louise Maynard." The thing in his hand wrote. "Probably the most beautiful of all. Intelligent too. More's the pity eh? If it were not for her tongue, her sharp, cutting, cruel tongue she would have outshone even Maurine wouldn't she? You watched what she did to men every week on her television show; baiting them, slicing them to ribbons in front of millions of people. A woman shouldn't do that to a man. Not a wholesome, intelligent girl like Louise. It was a terrible flaw in her. Oh, I'm not here to judge, Frank though I agree with you personally. I'm just here to exact payment, to execute (if you'll pardon my choice of words) the proceedings.

"Yes, she was a bitch alright. She won't be castrating any more men in front of network cameras though. You saw to that. You waited again Frank. In that bar across from the studio last night you worked up to it (though it took less and less of that everytime didn't it?) and contrived to share a taxi home with her. In the cab you were gentle in your admonitions. You were fair. You tried to explain to her what you were about to do and why it was it had to be done, why she was wrong. But then she called you that word. We know what it was. Remember now?

"And at five o'clock this morning standing on that darkened, windblown street with the trash eddying aroung like your thoughts in the freezing gusts, you plunged the knife squarely into her heart. Then you stabbed her everywhere else you could think of. Too bad she screamed before you thought to cut her throat, because she awakened someone on that street, someone just above the bookstore. He is one of our agents, we work for the same people and you have him to thank for our impending meeting. I am here at his bidding, at least for the moment. He thought we should get together. He was so right.

"Are you coming, Frank?"

The pen stopped moving abruptly. The room was silent save for the crash of heartbeats echoing crazily off of the walls and windows. Frank lifted the pen to the inkwell again, this time with his own muscle and will. There remained only a few drops of ink. He dabbed it onto the pen and touched the point to the bottom of the third card. He watched himself write, Season's Greetings.

And there was no more ink.

He stared at the cards before him all covered with the crowded handwriting in the scarlet ink and the words seemed to congeal into a puddle of blood. He listened with detachment to the erratic crescendo of some insane tympani, mounting, frenzied pagan drums. It was his heart. The pool of blood seemed to expand, engulf his vision. The world became a deep, achingly beautiful crimson.

And grew dark.

Deepening shades of red.

Pain in his chest, down his left arm. His right arm.

The world went black.

The drums stopped.

And for a long time there was nothing.

Three days elapsed before Frank Darby was discovered bent over his desk. It was Monday, the day after Christmas. His secretary let herself into the apartment with her keys that evening to look for some papers he had been carrying in his briefcase the previous Friday. She was somewhat annoyed at him for going off on one of his binges or to the islands or Europe without so much as a phone call. She also felt a little worried. It was not like him. He would have called drunk even at five in the morning, or from some airport thousands of miles away to let her know he was not coming in. She was afraid something might have happened. She didn't know what to think, but she did not expect to see his body, already putrefying, slumped over his desk. She called the police.

When they moved him they found a detailed confession to four slayings. It was there, on the desk beneath his dead weight and written on, of all things, Christmas cards, in red ink and apparently with an old fashioned type feather pen. The confessions contained information only the killer could have had, or the victims. The police were convinced. They stopped looking for "The Soho Strangler" and there were no more killings of that type. At least for a while, until the next psycho snapped somewhere in the city.

One did. They always do.

Oliver Ware, proprietor of The Lunar Light Occult Bookstore read accounts of the murders with relish. He began to assemble the things he would need. Green Silk, Hand of Glory, a volume by Hermes Trismegistus, blood of a murder victim, feather of a gryphon, things like that.

He smiled as he worked. He liked getting the right people together.

The City of Dread
By Lloyd Arthur Eshbach

The City Of Dread
by Lloyd Arthur Eshbach

The moon was a giant firefly caught in a web of cloud, its pallid light filtering dimly down to the narrow mountain trail. Stunted trees, leaning low over the path, rubbed leafy hands together with a mournful, rustling sound. Black shadows crouched under the overhanging branches. And over all loomed the towering peaks of the Peruvian *cordillera*, gashing the blue-black sky with jagged, blackened fangs.

A little caravan crawled warily up the narrow, winding trail—a woman, four men and their burros, one behind the other. The long, white beams of their electric torches, darting erratically among the gnarled trees, seemed to intensify the darkness. Uneasiness hung over the group, quelling speech. The last man, the *cholo* guide, leading the string of pack-animals, cast occasional hasty glances over his shoulder, watching little shadows steal silently from beneath the trees into patches of moonlight, bending and bowing and merging with the darkness.

"*Verdammte dummkopf!*" the second man in the column growled suddenly in a throaty Teutonic voice. "Why did we not stop for the night down in the valley as I suggested? It iss your fault, Marshall! *Ja,* you say, we reach the ruins before dark. We need but a climb a little while, and we are there! You said it, so it iss so!"

Ken Marshall, striding in the lead, looked down angrily at the shorter German. "Don't be childish, Ollendorpf!" he snapped in brittle tones. "I know it's my fault—but we may as well make the best of it. Anyway, we would have made it if we hadn't switched to the left back there at the fork. But you insisted that Enrique was wrong—so here we are." His voice became mockingly gentle. "I know you're afraid of the dark, Maxie—but I'll protect you. You're perfectly safe as long as I'm around."

"You protect me, *hein?*" the stocky German rumbled ominously. "It iss you who will need protection, Marshall, if you are not careful! I stand just so much—"

"That's enough, boys," Dr. J. Carlton Ashbery interposed quietly. "After all, as you pointed out, Kenneth, we're here—and we'll have to keep going till we reach Machu Picchu, for there's certainly no place to stop on this steep slope."

"Sorry, Doc," Marshall said in an altered voice. "I guess we really shouldn't have started. I was thinking of Peggy. What with those blood-sucking bats back there, and the snakes—"

Marguerite Ashbery interrupted in a clear, calm voice: "Don't worry about me, Ken. I'm all right. And forget the bats—they won't annoy us up here; it's too cold."

Ollendorph said nothing, though Marshall thought he heard a faint throaty, "Protect me, *hein?*"

After that there was a long silence. Only the breathless whisper of the wind and the sounds of their steady climbing broke the mountain-walled stillness.

Ken Marshall frowned, his thoughts disturbed. It wasn't bats that annoyed him—nor snakes—it was something else, something indefinable. Their trouble had started back at the mouth of the Urubamba Gorge. It was there that the *arrieros* had deserted.

They had camped on the river bank for the night, had gathered about the fire, and Dr. Ashbery had gotten out the little golden figure which had led them into the Andean highlands. It was a figure he had unearthed during an earlier visit to Machu Picchu, a grotesque gargoyle about six inches in height, wrought in the form of a squatting, bony-limbed man with an enormous bald head and hawk-beak nose.

Marshall had examined it with utmost care, fascinated by an artifact far above the recognized ability of any ancient American race. It was marvelously formed, a work of almost microscopic perfection. The leathery texture of the parchmentlike skin; the bulging, pouchy eyes, seeming about to open; the sunken cheeks, the thin, leering lips, tightly drawn over protruding teeth; the lean muscles and cordlike tendons—all were unbelievably perfect. It was almost as though he had held a gold plated mummy of a miniature man.

Despite its perfection—or perhaps because of it—Marshall had felt no admiration for the statuette. It seemed to be something abnormal, something which once had lived! And despite the absurdity of the thought, there still seemed to cling to the little figure a taint of unnatural life.

The Quichua packmen, at this, their first glimpse of the golden image, had gasped in awe, muttering fearfully the one word:

"Viracocha!"

Viracocha, the god of Chimus, a race more ancient than the Incas. The Creator of the moon and sun. The Lord of all Lords!

It was absurd, of course—but it had seemed that, with the half-heard mouthings of the Quichuas, that aura of unclean life had intensified. Light had seemed to flash from half-opened eyes—doubtless a reflection of the campfire—and the thin lips had seemed to part momentarily in a sardonic grin. Merely a flicker of the uncertain light, gone in a breath.

At dawn they had discovered the desertion of the *arrieros*. Only Enrique Fulano, the little half-breed guide, had remained. And that pall-like cloud of dread had settled upon all of them.

Ollendorph, particularly, had been affected. Naturally ill-tempered and morose, it had become an apparent impossibility for him to speak a civil word. Fervently Ken wished the German hadn't been invited to join the expedition, despite his knowledge of Peruvian antiquity.

Now they were on the last leg of their journey to Machu Picchu, the wonder city of the Incas. Cuzco lay sixty miles to the south; and somewhere above them in the darkness sprawled the ruins of a mighty city of cut and polished white granite, built more than two thousand years ago; a city, so legend said, from whence the first great Inca had come, and to which the last Inca King, Manco, had gone when fleeing the Spanish *conquistadors*. A city, it was whispered, which held the fabled, life-size golden statue of Huayna Capac, father of Atahualpa!

The final half mile of the climb was an age of lung-torturing effort. They climbed up steeply pitched slopes, stumbled through loose rubble, leaped over rain-washed gutters. As they topped the last steep rise, the guide exclaimed:

"Almost we are there, *senors!*"

A level path lay before them, and they felt the comparative smoothness of square-cut stones underfoot. An ancient Inca highway! They passed the last straggling clump of trees, and they saw a low white wall marking both sides of the road, its broken oblong slabs suggesting tombstones in the darkness. As they paused, the moon crept stealthily from behind a cloud bank and suddenly flooded the world with white light — and they saw Machu Picchu!

They stood on a level plateau, covered with a sparse growth of ichu grass. Before them and to the right rose steeply terraced stone walls. A flight of narrow stone steps along one wall led to the upper levels that extended tier upon tier above them. To the left and behind them lay sheer nothingness — a drop of a mile into the Urubamba Gorge! And over all brooded the somber mass of a great shadowed conical peak like a black cowled priest in eternal prayer. The threshold of Machu Picchu.

As suddenly as it had appeared, the moon vanished, and darkness fell. Only a rare, shivering star cast its lustre over the *cordillera*. In the gloom they could see nothing save faintly visible terraces of stone, like cyclopean steps on the mountainside, sheer expanses of white granite walls, and beyond, the black bulk of the mountain.

Lancelike, the waiting, sinister hush that enveloped the ruins intruded itself into Ken Marshall's consciousness. He felt a burden of inexpressible antiquity and desolation; the weight of ancient things pressed upon him, slowing his heartbeat. It was a place too old for the living, a city where only ghosts of ghosts might dwell.

"Well," Ollendorph growled, "why we wait?"

"We'll make camp right here till morning," Dr. Ashbery said quietly, swinging the beam of his flashlight in a wide circle, inspecting the terrain. "Enrique, you start a fire while we—"

His voice broke off and he stared queerly over the high stone wall. The others followed the direction of his gaze.

"I'd almost swear I saw a light," Ashbery said uncertainly.

Ken Marshall's eyes narrowed. There was a strange tension in the air that made breathing a conscious effort. He looked at blond haired Peggy Ashbery, clad like the men in leggings and breeches. She was leaning forward, staring in fascination. The flashlight winked into darkness, and for an instant the blackness seemed absolute.

"I see it—there it is!" Peggy exclaimed suddenly.

Ken frowned. He saw it too. There was a light

within Machu Picchu—but it was not a light that came from fire! Faint at first, it intensified as their eyes adjusted themselves to the gloom. It was a steady phosphorescent glow, like a light that might stream through a window, but a light that was cold, paper-white, and somehow ghastly!

Dr. Ashbery cleared his throat. "Probably some Quichuas," he said, but without conviction. Raising his voice, he shouted: "Hel-lo! Who's there?"

His cry echoed hollowly among the ruins, repeating itself into silence, but there was no other sound. Then again the moon shook free its cloak of cloud and cast its glow over Machu Picchu—and narrowed eyes scanned the skeleton city apprehensively. They saw no movement, no sign of life, nothing to disturb them save that uncanny, phosphorescent radiance.

"We'll have to investigate," Ashberry snapped at length, self-disgust in his manner. "If we don't, I suppose we'll huddle around the fire all night, frightened out of our silly wits. Kenneth and Max, suppose you go with me . . . Or, on second thought, Max, you stay here with Marguerite and Enrique. We'll be right back."

"*Ja!*" Ollendorph exclaimed with alacrity. "I guard Miss Peggy and the supplies."

As Marshall and the scientist, gripping their 30-30 Winchesters, turned toward the ancient city, Peggy involuntarily reached out a restraining hand, and a faint exclamation escaped her. Ken stopped short, and she lowered her hand.

"Oh—don't mind me," she said with an impatient little laugh. "A little scary, that's all."

Impulsively Marshall put his arm around her and

held her in a strong embrace. "Don't worry, Peg," he said gently. "We can take care of ourselves, and Max will be watching here. There's nothing to fear."

He released her; and the two men strode toward century-old Machu Picchu. With Marshall leading, they climbed the long stone stairway and entered the city. They paused for a moment, choosing a path through the tangle of underbrush that grew everywhere.

The light lay to their left at the top of a steep declivity. Broad stone walls blocked their way, walls and the ruins of roofless houses. The thick undergrowth, partly obscured by angular black shadows cast by the eery radiance and the light of the moon, made progress an apparent impossibility. This was a foolish trick, Ken thought ruefully, but they had little choice in the matter.

Cautiously they started in the general direction of the light. With every sense alert, they listened for unnatural sounds; watched for signs of life, for pitfalls which might lie in their path. Their progress was slow, but they hadn't a very great distance to cover; and gradually they approached their goal. As they neared the source of the radiance, Ken thought he detected a faint, musty, somewhat offensive odor in the air.

Ashbery's words came to him in a tense whisper. "I haven't seen any indication of life yet; have you, Kenneth?"

"Not a sign," Marshall replied, his tones low and unnatural. "The light seems to be coming from beneath that big slab of granite," he added — then stiffened into sudden rigidity.

A scream pierced the stillness! A scream of indescribable fear! Peggy's voice!

In the momentary paralysis that followed there was no other sound, no repetition of the scream. A breath—and Marshall tore madly back toward the stone stairway. He hurdled ancient walls, crashed through barriers of underbrush, skirting buildings recklessly. A choking fear throbbed in his throat, speeding his feet, guiding his course.

"Coming, Peg!" he shouted, his voice high and thin.

He reached the steps, raced down, rifle ready—and halted, stunned. There was no one there! Peggy, Ollendorpf, Enrique—gone. Only burros remained, bucking and kicking, fighting to wrench free from the saplings to which they were tethered. The burros and a lighted electric torch, resting on a clump of grass, pointing a rigid, futile finger of radiance into the clouded sky.

"Peggy!" he cried frantically. *"Peggy!"* There was no answer.

Then he saw Enrique, a dark mass lying prone beside a heap of unlighted faggots, and a black suspicion leaped into his mind. The German—had he knocked out the *cholo* and made off with Peggy—and Ashbery's image as well? He picked up the flashlight, turned it upon the burros. As though to confirm his suspicions, he saw the Professor's worn canvas saddle bag hanging open, its contents spilled out.

Enrique—if he were conscious, he could tell! He turned the half-breed over, stared into his face—and caught his breath in sudden, icy horror. Enrique was dead—but it was not death that froze Marshall's blood. It was the indescribable terror etched on the wide-eyed face, terror greater than human mind could bear, a dread nothing mortal could inspire. Dead—frightened to death! Shuddering, Marshall rolled him over on his face.

Impotently he gazed about him into the darkness, his lips thinned. Peggy in the power of a—thing—that could arouse such fear! Something welled up within him—rage, fear, a turmoil of rebellion—swelling, growing into a bursting, insane fury that must find outlet. His hands curled into knots at his sides; he sucked in a tremendous breath . . . And with an effort of will that was almost physical he held himself in check as Ashbery came panting up behind him. He forced back the surge of madness.

"What happened, Ken?" the scientist demanded in a hoarse, strained voice.

"It looks as though Ollendorpf has kidnapped Peggy," he replied evenly. "He must have slugged Enrique; he's—unconscious. And I'll bet your little statue is gone."

Mechanically Ashbery crossed to the burro bearing his saddlebags, held it steady with a firm hand and searched with the other. He turned away in a moment and nodded. "It's gone."

Then stunningly full realization of his greater loss swept over him. His face paled to a bloodless white; the cords of his neck stood out like vines on a tree; and his thin frame quivered with fury.

"Kenneth," he panted, "if—if he harms her, I'll—I'll—" He choked with emotion.

"Don't worry," Marshall consoled, the words a mockery in his own ears. "She'll be all right. He probably wants to hold her as hostage to make us leave and let him have clear sailing in his search for treasure." If it were only so! If he could only free his mind of its formless fears. But—he had seen the dead half-breed's face!

Dr. Ashbery pressed trembling fingers against his eyes; and Ken looked back over the ruins where the ghostly light still shone. Suddenly his hand fell on the professor's arm, viselike, and an unnatural stiffness crept over him. His lips whitened, and he gasped as though a hand of ice had clutched his throat. Hallucination—it must be hallucination!

Through the alternate night-black shadows and silver-gray moonlight of Machu Picchu stalked two powerful, dark-skinned forms. Birth-naked, they were, striding side by side, a fierce and haughty pride in their posture. Clearly he saw them—but just as clearly he saw the bone-white walls and shadowed undergrowth behind them! Transparent!

Dimly Marshall heard Ashbery's halting words: "I—I'm losing—my mind!"

Now the two wraith-like figures reached the top of the steps and began to descend. Ken saw their faces; and he shuddered with instinctive revulsion. Masks of utter evil—of vicious cruelty. Essentially the features were alike; the eyes, wide apart and carbon-black, glittering with eager desire . . . the noses, hawk-sharp, dilated hungrily . . . the mouths, wide, thin-lipped, drooping. They paused before the stiffly waiting men.

The lips of one moved with soundless speech; and his words, in the tongue of the ancient Incas, impressed themselves upon Marshall's mind.

"You take the old one, Apu Tintaya. I will possess

the younger."

Like swooping bats they leaped! Ashbery screamed; and with a fearfilled curse Ken struck out wildly, blindly with both fists. Flailed through emptiness. Then something enveloped him, something that clung as mist might cling — cold mist, damp, marrow-chilling. A mist that smothered, that seemed to flow into his nostrils, that tore at his consciousness.

In desperation Marshall struggled against an insidious numbness that crept into his brain. What — what were these things? The ghosts of long-dead Incas? Phantoms? But these phantoms were terribly real, else he would not feel this growing weight, this strangely material something that seemed to be merging with his own personality.

If — if he could but think! If he could fix his mind upon one thing, could check this flickering of his reason. Alien thoughts were creeping into his brain — savage thoughts — flashes of memory that could not be his own.

The booming throb of a huge serpent-skin drum, rolling over a silent multitude . . . The wild chant of naked, blood-smeared priests . . . The lurid light of an altar flame glittering on a slab of polished obsidian and the naked form of a maiden cruelly outstretched for the sacrifice . . . The flash of a knife that had drunk the blood of thousands . . . A single agonized scream mingling with the shuddering cry of the populace . . . A stalwart, crimson-splotched figure triumphantly holding aloft a throbbing, dripping heart . . . And above all the moaning of the spirits of the upper air, echoing the voices of the countless dead whose hearts had been torn from them on that accursed spot . . .

A shudder shook Ken Marshall—a shudder that became a continuous thing, convulsions wracking his frame. His chest swelled mightily; his muscles knotted in agony; he writhed in torment. His thoughts were chaotic, incoherent, his resistance weakening, being thrust back . . . Hell! He must resist—must keep his senses to help Peggy!

Peggy! Out of desperation came new strength. He felt a tingling shock. The winds of chaos died in his brain. And abruptly he was master of himself, his mind keenly awake, every inch of him taut with frigid fury. No damned spirit could claim his body for its own use! Strongly he resisted now—resisted with implacable determination—and suddenly knew that he alone was tenant of his mind.

Before him crouched the wraith-like Inca, snarling with voiceless rage. And his eyes—his eyes glared greenly, like the night-eyes of a wolf! A soundless, malignant whisper came to Marshall:

"Now is victory yours—but Atahualpa will return!"

Atahualpa! Momentary consternation checked thought and breath and heartbeat. Atahualpa—most heartless of all the Inca Kings—mad Atahualpa, drinker of his brothers' blood! . . . Through a shadowy haze that crept stealthily before his vision, Ken Marshall watched the phantom turn and stalk up the stone steps into Machu Picchu. Beside him strode the tall, lean form of Dr. J. Carlton Ashbery. Of the specter called Apu Tintaya there was no trace.

Dumbly, without thought, Marshall watched them till they disappeared among the ruins, watched till the ghastly phosphorescence vanished, and silent, pitchy darkness fell. Mercifully, his senses left him.

The pallid face of dawn peered over the eastern mountains when Ken Marshall opened his eyes. Shivering with cold, he stared blankly into a low-hanging bowl of gloomy, gray-white cloud. Slowly he struggled to his feet, sharp pain piercing every muscle in his body. He stood there swaying, trying to think.

He turned at a sound behind him—the flap of dismal wings—and his lips curled with revulsion at the spectacle he beheld. Four loathsome vultures almost covered that which had been Enrique Fulano, rending and tearing the flesh of the faithful guide. Angrily Ken caught up a heavy rock and heaved it toward the scavengers.

"Get out, you damned carrion eaters!" he shouted, staggering toward them, his arms flailing. One hand brushed against his holster and he dragged out his Colt .44 and fired at the reeking birds. Feathers flew; and three of the vultures flapped into the air, croaking their displeasure. The fourth flopped about disgustingly, its head a bloody ruin.

"You'll get no more of him," Marshall rasped, firing skyward—then stopped short before the ghastly cadaver with its gleaming expanses of fleshless bone. His eyes widened with horror and a shudder shook him. He scowled uncertainly. Something had killed the breed—and he should remember what it was—but he felt foggy, his head stuffed with cotton.

Clenching his teeth, Marshall stopped and caught up the dreadful remains, flinging the body across his shoulder. He didn't have the strength to bury the guide—couldn't seem to think straight—but, by damn, Enrique had been faithful — and he'd see to it that he didn't fill the bellies of a flock of vultures!

Struggling against the strange weakness that set his legs to trembling, he staggered across the rough terrain to the edge of the plateau, pausing on the brink of a chasm that fell sheerly for a mile into the Urubamba River. The table of rock seemed to have been cleft by a mighty downward sweep of a titanic machete. He stood swaying on the edge of destruction, staring at a frozen sea of cloud a hundred feet below him, filling all the valley with motionless gray-white billows through which jutted, jagged, islandlike peaks.

With a sudden, spasmodic heave he flung the body from him — stepped back, stood wide-legged, watching as it plummeted into the cloud-sea and disappeared. For an instant he waited, straining his ears unconsciously for the crash of its landing — then snorted in self-disgust. The sound of the crash could never reach this height. Turning, in the same half-stupor which had held him since his awakening, he moved back toward the pack animals. Stood there, pressing his hands over his eyes, trying to think.

Suddenly his mind was alive with thoughts, thoughts scurrying about aimlessly, jostling each other, thoughts fighting for supremacy, wild thoughts hammering at the inner walls of his skull. The preceeding night — the light in Machu Picchu — Peggy's scream — that strange, strange fight with a wraith-like combatant who called himself — Atahualpa! Bloody Atahualpa, slayer of two hundred of his kin, so that he might be the only one of the royal line left alive! That dreadful vision of bloody sacrifice . . . Then the strange departure of Professor Ashbery and *one* wraith . . . Imagination? He shook his head. It had happened!

Peggy—where was Peggy? In the power of such as— Atahualpa? Perhaps possessed by a long-dead demon as was her father? Weakness that was more than physical surged through Ken Marshall, weakness and impotent horror. What could he do?

His gaze swept over Machu Picchu, inspecting the walled enclosures, mounting stone-lined terraces where gardens once had been, picking out palaces, temples, shrines, baths and fountains. A marvel city, perched on a mountaintop, with the razorback peaks and terra cotta flanks of the Andes for a setting. A marvel city, but a city shrouded in the dust of death— a city overshadowed by a cloud of dread.

His eyes halted on what appeared to be a great flat boulder on the crest of a steep, terraced slope. It was from beneath that granite slab that the light had come—he was certain of it! Perhaps more than light! And perhaps beneath it his friends had gone!

With feverish energy Marshall sprang forward toward the steps that led into Machu Picchu—and stumbled on limbs that almost buckled beneath him. "Hell!" he rasped aloud. There was no reason for such weakness. It took more than a night of exposure to the dampness and cold of the Andean highlands to knock him out. It must have been the fight—that hellish fight with—something—which had drained the strength from his body.

Gritting his teeth, he moved cautiously up the steps into the ancient city. Through the ruins he made his way, ignoring the marvelous masonry which thrust through the underbrush on every side. He had eyes only for the great white slab, an immense mass of granite which must have weighed tons, one of the sacred stones of the Incas.

As he drew close he saw irregular heaps of uprooted brush and raw earth bordering the slab on every side, and he pressed forward eagerly, certain that the slab must have been moved only hours ago. He reached it and bent over, scanning the edges where it rested upon a low wall of smoothly cut stones. His heart sank. No light could have come from beneath this boulder. Nor could anyone have entered the burial cave that probably lay beneath it, for merely to move it would require the combined strength of a score of men.

About to turn away, he leaned over swiftly, staring wide-eyed. There, clinging to the roughened edge of a crack in the masonry, were several strands of long, silken, blond hair! Peggy's hair—caught as if dragged across the stone! Pinched beneath the great slab!

Slowly he straightened with the golden threads between his fingertips. She was down there in the pit under the stone! The thing had been moved once—and it could be moved again! Crouching, he ran his fingers along the edge, seeking a hold beneath the slab. He found it; and even as he began to tug, the muscles of his legs gave way and he half-sprawled across the rock.

In the grip of bitter, impotent rage, Marshall drew himself erect. For dragging moments he stood on wide-spread legs, panting, his balled fists dangling helplessly at his sides. What could he do? He *must* do something . . . Better get a grip on himself and get back his strength before he did anything else.

Resolutely he turned away from the stone slab and plodded through the ruins, back toward the burros.

He found the pack animals where he had left them, contentedly chewing the sparse ichu grass. He watered them; then built a fire and hastily prepared food for himself. He forced himself to eat and to drink, though the food was as tasteless as ashes in his mouth. The black coffee he brewed was most welcome; it drove the icy chill from his bones and set his blood to coursing freely through his body. He was almost himself again as he prepared to return to the slab of rock.

Carefully he inspected his revolver, slipping cartridges into the empty chambers. He hung a canteen of water from his belt beside his flashlight, and with a pick and shovel over his shoulder, strode back through the city.

As he approached the mass of granite, Marshall closed his mind to everything but the task at hand. He inspected the great stone with utmost care, noting every detail, particularly interested in the low wall that supported it. Half buried though it was by the accumulated humus of centuries, he believed that through the wall lay a means of entrance. He fell to work and in a very short time he cleared away sufficient earth to expose a yard-wide section of the wall. Like all Chimu masonry, the smoothly polished stones were fitted together without cement or mortar, the artisans depending upon the perfection of their work to keep their walls standing.

Selecting a spot close to the place where he had found Peggy's hair, and where a root had created a gap in the masonry, Ken attacked the wall. The stones resisted stubbornly, as though wedged into place; he labored interminably to remove the first stone. With that accomplished at last, the other stones left their resting place with surprising ease; within minutes he had cleared a space large enough to admit his body.

With every sense alert and with muscles taut, he stopped and turned the beam of his electric torch into the opening. A flight of ancient, footworn stone steps fell away below him, curving into a hidden corridor barely suggested by the light of his flash. A dank and peculiarly odorous current of air rose from the depths, whispering through the aperture into Marshall's face. The unnatural cold momentarily chilled him, causing him to hesitate; but an instant later, with a final glance at the ancient city behind him and with the beam lighting his way, he crawled head first into the opening.

It was damp within the passageway, damp and clammily cold, and that odor of musty antiquity filled the air. Dust lay thickly upon the hollowed steps — and with sudden mingled jubilation and dread, Marshall saw a confusion of footprints extending before him down the stairs. He arose to his feet, crouching under the great slab, then pressed forward eagerly, his forty-four clutched in one hand and the flashlight in the other.

The stairway ended, and a high arched corridor lay before him, sloping gently downward. He swept the smooth walls with his light, then moved swiftly forward, following the footprints in the dust.

For several hundred feet Marshall strode through an incredible tunnel hewn into the solid rock of the mountain. Despite the tension that gripped him, despite his anxiety, he could not help but marvel at the prodigious effort and the amazing skill which had gone into the construction of this ancient corridor. He marveled, too, at the smoothly polished grooves in the stone floor, worn by the passage of countless feet. Only constant use during scores of centuries could have worn such depressions in the hard granite floor.

He reached the end of the corridor; and the footprints stopped at the edge of a second great slab of stone. But unlike the other, this mass of granite rested directly upon the floor of the passageway! Here were no stones which could be pried loose to provide entrance.

With sinking heart Marshall examined the barrier. Was he to be stopped here when Peggy might be imprisoned just beneath that slab? He stood there for dragging minutes, raging inwardly at his complete helplessness. His light played over every inch of the granite block, seeking anything that might suggest a way to force passage under the slab. Useless! Impotently he dropped to a seat on the block, his elbows resting upon his knees, his head drooping.

As he sat there, the utter soundlessness and the shadow filled blackness weighed upon him. It was as though great evil had been done in this place, and as though the influence of the evil survived in the darkness and silence. That fetid odor of antiquity seemed to be more intense, and the shadows that writhed just beyond the edge of his beam seemed to be sentient, alive. Almost it seemed that inhuman presences lurked there, incorporeal entities waiting patiently just beyond the radiance. Not wraiths of Incas—formless elemental things. In spite of himself, Marshall felt a faint chill tingling along his spine.

Abruptly he sprang to his feet, his expression savage. Letting his imagination go like that! A bad case of nerves. Yet, despite every effort, he could not rid himself of the uneasy feeling that he was not completely alone. No amount of rational thinking could change it. Some disembodied intelligence seemed to be hovering above him, aware of his thoughts—mocking his despair! Almost he could sense a sneering, wordless invitation to enter the place beneath the slab, to continue his quest. Furiously Marshall rasped into the shadows:

"Open the way, damn you—and I'll enter!"

As though in direct answer, the mighty stone shook, and slowly rose as on a hinge to a position perpendicular with the wall! Hung there, sustained by an invisible power! And mocking, jeering laughter seemed to echo through Marshall's brain.

Soundlessly came the words: "The way—is open."

For moments Ken crouched as though stunned. Thought itself ceased. Then fear struck deeply— blind, unreasoning, irrational fear—but before terror could overwhelm him, before he could think about what had happened, he sprinted down the steps!

Desperately he fought for control of his reeling reason. He—he didn't give a damn what had raised that stone! It had moved—and he had his chance to find Peggy and Ashbery and Ollendorpf. And although the musty odor had increased now beyond any intensity it had previously attained, he managed to close his mind against terror and the thought of his fearful position. He closed his consciousness to everything but that which lay ahead.

He stood at the threshold of a tremendous vault. As

his beam circled the chamber, a gasp burst from him and he stood motionless, incredulous wonder thrusting the last vestige of fear far into the background. Before him lay the treasure of the Incas, a portion of the wealth which was to have ransomed Atahualpa, but which had never been delivered to Pizarro. A treasure to drive men mad.

For minutes Marshall's eyes roved over the glittering mass piled in a disordered heap on the smooth flat top of a great, rounded, table-like stone. Raw gold in nuggets and dust — gold ornaments and vessels — uncut gems flashing smoldering crimson and green and deep blue fire in the light of his torch. And over all towered a huge golden image, half buried in the incredible mound — the fabled statue of the Inca King, Huayna Capac!

Sharply Marshall shook his head. Time enough to think of treasure after he'd found Peggy and the rest. Resolutely he turned his beam away from the gleaming pile and circled the man-made cavern. The fan-shaped ray revealed a place of staggering proportions — a smooth stone ceiling twenty feet above his head — curved walls enclosing a circular room a hundred feet or more in diameter! A drum-shaped vault hewn from the solid rock of the Andes!

Darkly shadowed niches marred the smoothness of the walls, rounded openings about three feet wide, circling the wall at ten foot intervals — niches, breast-high, that stared like empty, lidless eyes. Cautiously Marshall approached the nearest opening — and now he saw that it was not empty, that it contained a grisly tenant, the parchment-dry, mummified body of an Inca priest!

As he stared into the crypt, the white light of his flash revealing every ghastly detail of the ancient cadaver, Marshall's lip curled with revulsion, and consciousness of the musty odor, the soundless dark, swept over his senses. There was something hideously lifelike in the position of the leather-brown figure, squatting on fleshless haunches with skeletal arms wrapped around bony legs in the customary manner of Inca burial. Little remained of the gorgeous trappings which had once adorned the royal body; the slow decay of uncounted centuries had crumbled the brilliant robes to dust, leaving only the ornaments of gem-encrusted gold. Metal and mummified flesh alone had resisted the gnawing teeth of Time.

Methodically, with emotions and imagination held rigidly in check, Marshall inspected each of the crypts. Twenty-three there were in all, the first lying to the left of the stairway, the last equi-distant from the right side. And in each squatted the mummy of an ancient Inca king or priest!

As he moved slowly from crypt to crypt, examining each to be certain that Peggy might not lie bound within, Marshall observed that the mummies seemed progressively to be in a better state of preservation; when he reached the last—the figure that must have been Atahualpa—the body was fearsomely lifelike, fully clad in the garments of nobility . . . He became aware of something else, too, a vague and formless impression that persisted in forcing itself upon his consciousness. His mind groped for understanding —and abruptly he knew—knew while he scoffed at a conviction that was utterly fantastic.

Life clung to each age-stiffened corpse—life that

was evil, unnatural, and infinitely more dreadful than death!

As he gazed at the once-powerful form of Atahualpa, Ken thought of Dr. Ashbery and of Apu Tintaya, the Priest who had possessed the archeologist's body. And suddenly another thought came, a question of vast importance, but one he could not answer. Did the Incas, when they gained new bodies, permit these shriveled hulks to disintegrate, or did they hold intact the ties which bound them to their corpses? If those bonds *were* severed, it meant that Ashbery—and perhaps Peggy and Ollendorpf—were permanently possessed by the spirits of savage Incas! His brow furrowed. He could only hope that possession was temporary. He grimaced. No use thinking about that now. Finding them was his first consideration.

Impatiently he sent the rays of his electric torch over the floor, the walls and the ceiling, searching for the doorway he felt he must have missed. Those he sought could not be in this chamber. He saw nothing unusual save a small, square opening, about a foot high, in the wall directly opposite the stairway. He had missed it at first because it was above the level of his vision.

Standing on tiptoe, Marshall saw the grotesque figure of Viracocha squatting in the niche—the same statuette which had led them into Machu Picchu!

Eagerly he grasped the gargoyle, and as he touched it, it slid back as though in a groove—and smoothly, silently, the granite wall before him parted from floor to ceiling and slowly slid aside! He felt the little image sliding away with the wall, and mechanically he let go. A doorway opened into a long, stone-walled corridor curving gently before him into hazy semi-darkness.

Semi-darkness! There must be light ahead! With swift eagerness he flung himself into the corridor—then stopped short as a faint sound reached his ears. He crouched motionless, listening intently, and faintly through the passageway came the subdued hum of voices! Marshall's flashlight blinked into darkness, and he waited, nerves wire-taut. Now the voices came more clearly, but they were too indefinite for recognition or understanding.

As his eyes grew accustomed to the gloom, Marshall felt his skin crisping. There *was* light ahead—a pallid, sickish glow, identical, except for intensity, with the light he had seen in Machu Picchu! The luminosity waxed and waned at irregular intervals, as though it might be the glow of a hidden altar fire.

Cautiously Marshall started down the passageway, guided by the faint light ahead. His electric torch might reveal his presence; he clipped it to his belt. As he advanced, Marshall felt with increasing force the formless menace that lurked in the very air of the place. It was as though something completely alien, something incredibly ancient, something hideously alive, dwelt amid these subterranean vaults, infusing everything with its unholy life. As though he were approaching the source of evil! He thought of the granite slab which had seemed to move of its own volition, of silent, scornful laughter, and he felt a momentary stab of fear. He shook his head rebelliously. He was letting the place get on his nerves again.

The voices reached him more clearly now, and

Marshall hesitated, listening—heard Ollendorpf's guttural growl and Ashbery's treble, both talking in the Inca tongue. There came another voice, a low cry that sent Ken racing recklessly down the sloping corridor toward the source of the luminosity.

Peggy's voice, hushed, terrified, pleading: "Dad— Max—don't please! You're—you're mad!"

Even as he ran, Marshall heard the old scientist utter Inca words that could not belong to him: "A fitting sacrifice to Viracocha, as you suggest, Huayna Capac."

The rumbling tones of Max Ollendorpf made some reply, but to Ken Marshall came only a meaningless blur of sounds. Ahead lay a great cone-shaped chamber flooded with that ghastly light. And within it were Peggy, and the things which had been Dr. Ashbery and Max Ollendorpf, the German crouching over the bound form of the girl. Grotesque figures, clad in the tattered splendor of ancient Inca robes, put on over shirts and breeches.

Now they heard him; and the men whirled. A savage cry burst from Ollendorpf, followed by a torrent of Incan fury. From beneath the frayed folds of his cloak he whipped out a murderous bronze blade with a saw-toothed edge, and held it ready.

In apparent heedlessness, Ken charged—but when it seemed he must impale himself upon the weapon, he sprang off to one side and crashed with lowered head full into the midriff of the old scientist. Ashbery dropped with a gasping groan. Ken righted himself in time to side-step the charge of the German, avoiding the down-sweep of the sword by a hairbreadth. He darted in, swinging a short, powerful, chopping blow that struck Ollendorpf's wrist—that sent his blade spinning through the air in a wide arc.

They thudded against each other, groping for holds. The German's arms whipped around Marshall's waist, and his bulky body thrust against him, bending him backward. Savagely Ken drove his knee into Ollendorpf's groin, wrenching free as the powerful grip loosened and the Teuton stifled a groan. Marshall's fist lashed to the point of the other's jaw, a glancing blow that served only to infuriate him. He leaped in again—and Marshall met his charge with a powerful right to the pit of his stomach.

A howl ripped from Ollendorpf, and he doubled with agony, gasping for breath. Again Ken swung, a powerful uppercut with all his weight behind it, a blow that lifted the Teuton and dropped him to the floor, as limp as an empty sack.

Marshall stepped back—and out of the corner of his eye he caught a glimpse of stealthy movement. He whirled, dodged a vicious cut of the bronze sword, and his fist thudded against the lean jaw of J. Carlton Ashbery. His head snapped back and he collapsed without a sound.

Panting, his face flushed, his heart hammering, Ken turned to the girl.

"Ken!" The word came from Peggy's pallid lips in a horrified gasp. "Ken—you too!"

He shook his head and smiled reassuringly. "No, Peggy—I'm still all right. Your father and Max—they're not themselves. But we'll get 'em out of this somehow." He picked up the blade Ollendorpf had dropped, and as he cut the cords that bound the girl, he kept up a smooth flow of words.

"It's a temporary derangement, I think, Peggy — sort of demon possession. A Jeckyl-Hyde affair — with Hyde in the driver's seat. It's bad, I'll admit, but after we get them out of this place I think they'll come around all right."

He lifted her to her feet, and for a moment held her tightly in his arms. A tremor shook her slim form, and abruptly she hid her face against his chest, her taut nerves and long-restrained emotions giving way to uncontrolled sobs. Let her cry, Marshall thought; best thing that could happen to her. A safety valve. Too much had happened in too short a time, and she'd come close to the breaking point.

She quieted finally and looked up into his face, attempting a smile. Gently he kissed the lips so close to his own, then released her.

"There'll be no more of that," she said. "The tears, I mean! What must we do now?"

Marshall frowned. "We've got to get out of here — all of us — and as quickly as possible. But first we'd better tie your dad and Ollendorpf, just to avoid trouble."

He caught up the cord that had bound the girl and crouched over the flaccid figure of the German. As he tied his hands behind him, he became aware of his nearness to the source of the strange radiance, and he felt his flesh crawl. In the heat of action he had not noticed it, but now the chill menace of the — Presence within this chamber struck deep. He fought against an urge to glance over his shoulder, compelled himself to finish binding the wrists and ankles of the German. Finally he thrust the strange bronze sword beneath his belt and arose.

His eyes sought Peggy's—and he stiffened as he saw the terror in her gaze—saw the fear etched upon her face by the unearthly, phosphorescent glow. He followed the direction of her blue eyes; saw for the first time whence the unnatural radiance came.

The room itself was a cylinder capped by a huge inverted cone, its point rising high above their heads. About six feet from the floor the ends of the cone straightened to drop vertically. And from a six foot area of this wall, directly in line with the entrance to the corridor, poured the strange luminescence. That in itself was not terrifying—it was the suggestion of something alive within the square of light that awakened dread.

A veil cloaked the square—a shimmering veil that only half concealed what lay behind it. What it was, he could not say—but it was evil—terribly evil. For an instant he thought he saw a gigantic counterpart of the little squatting image of Viracocha, but he couldn't be sure. No image, this—something alive— and something so hideous that it struck his sensibilities like a blow. Yet it was something that lured—lured with a promise of power—of desire fulfilled.

A faint, whimpering cry came from Peggy, and she buried her face in her hands. "Let's go, Ken—before it's too late."

Marshall nodded, his throat dry. "You head through the corridor and I'll follow with your father. I'll have to come back for Max."

Raising the lank form of Dr. Ashbery to his shoulder, he followed the girl across the room into the hallway. Briskly, almost in panic, they hurried along its curving length, Marshall's electric torch lighting the way. Behind them semi-darkness closed in as they approached the end of the corridor—and suddenly they stopped short.

The passageway ended in a blank wall of stone!

"I left that open when I came in," Ken exclaimed, a tremor in his voice despite his rigid control. "Must have slid shut automatically." He let his burden slide to the floor and moved close to the barrier, examining it with the aid of his flashlight.

"This thing should open from the inside," he said casually. "We'll just have to strike the right combination."

Apparently there *was* no right combination, Ken had to admit after a thorough but futile search. The way to the outside world was closed! He turned to Peggy Ashbery, putting a strong arm around her shoulders.

"Peggy, dear," he said gently, "we're in a jam. For the present we're trapped. But you can bet there's a way out, or the two Incas, in the persons of your father and Ollendorpf, wouldn't be in here."

The girl's eyes widened and her face grew pallid. Momentarily she held her breath, then laid a strong, slender hand on Marshall's arm.

"There'll be some way out, Ken," she said quietly. "I just know it." She paused, then gestured toward his canteen, forcing a faint smile. "I'm thirsty."

After she had drunk she continued, "Did I hear you mention two Incas?"

"I meant your father and Ollendorpf." Briefly Marshall explained, describing the macabre attack at the gateway of Machu Picchu. The girl listened with rapt, horrified fascination.

"At this moment, Peg, that isn't your father there on the floor. It's his body, but except for physical appearance, that's Apu Tintaya, an Inca Priest whose body died five hundred years ago! Whose ego-spirit if you prefer — has been bound to his mummy during all these years. And Max Ollendorpf is Huayna Capac, a King who lived during the same period. I'd rather not tell you things so dreadful, Peggy, but you should know so you can understand why they are as they are."

After a pause he went on slowly: "There's something else. I may be crossing a bridge that won't need crossing, but — well, I think we'd better be ready for anything. I mentioned my struggle with Atahualpa — and you may depend on it, Peggy, he hasn't given up. He wants my body! Maybe next time I won't be strong enough to resist. If he does take over, you won't be safe with any of us."

Quickly he unbuckled his gun belt and fastened it around the girl's slender waist, drawing it up as tightly as he could. "If necessary, Peggy," he admonished earnestly, "use it!"

A faint sound drifting along the corridor from the conical room terminated the conversation for the moment. With a glance at the supine form of Ashbery to assure himself that he still was unconscious, Ken thrust the flashlight into Peggy's hand, flung a quick, "I'll be right back," over his shoulder, and darted down the passageway.

As he reached the light-filled chamber, Marshall stopped short in consternation. The room was empty!

Ollendorpf had vanished!

Uncertainly Marshall entered the room, his eyes fixed on the luminous veil. The German must have gone behind that vaporous barrier; there was no other place to go. But how—bound as he was . . .

The thought was arrested by the husky form of Ollendorpf savagely charging out of the shimmering light, arms spread wide, fingers clawlike, lips drawn back. Ken's hand flashed to his side, and even as he remembered he had given Peggy the revolver, he flung himself prone before the onrushing Teuton. One upflung hand caught a booted ankle in midair as Ollendorpf leaped, and he crashed heavily to the floor. Marshall scrambled swiftly erect; but the German lay where he had fallen, stunned.

Ken spun toward the veil of light. Ollendorpf could not have gone behind that veil, could not have freed himself without help! Yet there was no sound, no sign of movement. With hair prickling, he stood motionless, waiting for he knew not what.

At length he turned, his lips framing a silent curse. This was getting his nerve—and he couldn't deny it. He couldn't take a chance on investigating the square of light—not with Peggy to look out for. With some difficulty he lifted the heavy frame of Ollendorpf to his shoulder and lumbered back through the corridor.

He found the girl waiting almost as he had left her. "What was wrong, Ken?" she asked tensely.

He shook his head. "Nothing much. Maxie—or Huayna Capac—had come to, and he'd managed to free himself. I had to put him to sleep again. And now I'm going to fix him so he'll stay safe for a while."

Dropping the limp form, he ripped aside the ragged robe and drew the heavy belt from the German's breeches. He buckled this around him, pinning his arms to his back with blood-stopping pressure.

Without comment he secured the older man in the same manner.

Rising, he said casually, "Now, Peg, we've got to play a waiting game. Unless I'm badly mistaken, in a little while this door will slide open, all of its own accord. You remember when we first saw the light in Machu Picchu? I'm certain it came from back there in the cone. When it passed through, it must have had clear passage—so it's a pretty safe bet that this door will open when the big slab rises. And when it does, we'll make a quick exit."

There followed for the man and girl an interminable period of waiting. Conversation between them was sporadic and forced. Among other things they spoke of Peggy's experience after Marshall and Ashbery had left to investigate the strange light. Ollendorpf, busying himself with the packs, had surreptitiously taken out the little golden figure of Viracocha. The girl had objected, sharply remonstrating—had tried to seize it—and suddenly the image had seemed to come to life, swelling to gigantic proportions, glowing with an unholy light— seeming to leap upon the two. Peggy had screamed— had fainted—and had awakened many hours later in the cone-shaped room, bound, and in the presence of her strangely maddened father and the German.

During their vigil, the two trussed men awakened, but they made no sound. Only their eyes moved, glaring at Marshall with savage wrath.

And repeatedly during that nerve-wracking period of waiting, Marshall's glance turned toward the end of the corridor, his thoughts dwelling uneasily on what might lie behind the curtain of light. He thought of all that had transpired since they had reached the ancient city, and he wondered what the end might be.

Then at last they heard a faint swishing sound—the way to freedom lay open—and a veritable torrent of cold light flooded the corridor and the vault beyond!

"Quick, Peggy!" Marshall caught her hand and together they sprang into the treasure chamber. He heard the two trussed men struggling to their feet; and even as he whirled toward the edge of the doorway where the golden figure of Viracocha squatted in its niche, they sprang through the opening and darted across the room. Ignoring them, Ken seized the little figure and wrenched at it with all his strength. It came away in his grasp and the door slid shut! Closed against whatever life-form lay within.

Blackness fell, thick, oppressive, utter blackness. For a tense, timeless instant Marshall stood rigid, Peggy's fingers gripping his arm. Then he cut the darkness with the beam of his electric torch.

"Outside!" he cried, flashing his light toward the stairway, momentarily outlining the professor and Ollendorpf—and the ray winked out! Total darkness fell. Frantically Marshall fumbled with the flashlight, shook it, strove to secure light.

"What's wrong, Ken?" Peggy's voice shook.

"The light's gone haywire," Marshall grated. "Loose connection or dead battery. We'll have to feel our way along the wall. Just hang onto my arm. We'll get out."

He clipped the flash to his belt, and suddenly realized that he still held the little golden image. Slipping it into a pocket of his breeches, he began moving along the curving stone wall, feeling his way with outthrust hands. He reached the nearest crypt—and in spite of himself, halted, his eyes boring through the darkness. Involuntarily he stepped back, his eyes narrowed to slits.

There was movement there—movement, invisible, soundless, yet movement that struck his senses with an unmistakable impact. He heard Peggy's sharp intake of breath, and he gritted his teeth. His hand fell to the hilt of the Inca sword hanging at his side and he gripped it strongly.

He moved ahead slowly, soundlessly—then paused again. For now he *saw*—saw, though there was no lessening of the blackness! Saw vaporous figures emerging from the black mouths of the crypts! Was aware of soundless voices within his own mind—the ghost-voiced whispering of the wraiths!

"Ken—look!" Peggy's gasp quivered with dread. Marshall spun around—saw almost upon him the familiar cloudlike shade of Atahualpa! Without realizing he did so, he swept up the bronze blade and swung it viciously—felt it pass unretarded through the phantom. And the thing was upon him, seeking to possess his body! Again he felt that clammy, smothering, vaporous something writhing into his nostrils, filling his lungs, tearing at his brain.

Fear surged through Marshall, bitter, icy fear. And weary—Lord, he was weary. He pressed his clenched fists into his eye sockets. How numb his brain felt! A haziness crept around his mind like a cold, dank fog, dripping fog, alive, writhing through the cells of his brain. Despair, black despair swept over his heart in a ponderous tide, constricting about his throat, over-whelming him. And hatred, mad hatred boiled in his brain, hell-spawned hatred, deadly malevolence, all consuming . . .

Whence came this hatred? Who was it he hated so? . . . *Who but those of his kin, his forbearers who dared to cling to life when he had willed that they die! He, Atahualpa, was greatest of all—and he alone should live again!*

Atahualpa drew in a tremendous breath and flexed his newly claimed body from head to foot. It was good to have form of flesh and blood after the unnumbered moons in this cave of death! Good to feel again the surge of life. As it had been in the olden days, so would it be again. Blood would flow and men would know the power of Atahualpa. But first—there must be none to question his right to rule!

A mighty shout burst from Atahualpa and he swung aloft the blade in his hand. From first to last would they die, body and spirit—these others who clung to life when they should be dead. None could prevent, not even the Lord of Lords . . . He sprang across the chamber through the blackness toward the place of burial where crouched the first great King . . . Light? He needed no light who so long had seen with the sight of the mind.

His hand swept into the night-black opening and brought forth a crumbling, skeletal thing—flung it aloft—slashed through it with his mighty blade—stamped it underfoot . . . With a wordless, eery cry in which was mingled hatred and savage exultation, that which had been Ken Marshall sprang to the next crypt—swept it clean of its grisly tenant—hacked the mummy to fragments with the saw-toothed sword . . . Moved on to the next crypt, howling with insensate laughter. Destroyed the ancient corpse . . . On to the next . . .

A ghostly horde circled and swirled about the head of Atahualpa—beating upon it with fists of fog—screaming soundless entreaties—begging, cursing—vanishing . . . For with each mummy destroyed was freed the tomb-bound spirit of another Inca.

Dust arose to fill the great chamber with a choking cloud, fetid, odorous dust that clogged the nostrils and throat of Atahualpa, thickening his cry. But with rending hand and hacking sword, he strode from crypt to crypt, destroying all in his path.

He came at length to the tomb of Apu Tintaya—the Priest who had shared his power—and through the crimson haze of hatred he saw crouched the unmoving figure of a white skinned maiden. Momentarily he halted—then with a powerful stroke of his arm he swept her aside and swung his blade into the corpse of Apu Tintaya. Felt it cleave the skeletal torso from shoulder to groin . . . Then stood as one paralyzed, the blade slipping from unfeeling fingers. Stood while the personality of Ken Marshall reasserted itself.

Ken Marshall stared dumbly into blackness, striving to awaken his mind to thought. He remembered the second attack of Atahualpa—his fear . . . Then overwhelmingly he remembered other things, alien thoughts and savage, unnatural ambitions which had belonged to Atahualpa. Atahualpa, who had conquered him, had possessed his body!

But why was he free now?

He heard a faint moan near at hand. Peggy! Perhaps he—or Atahualpa—had hurt her! He remembered having swept her aside. He groped around him, seeking her.

"Peggy!" he called. "Peggy!" there was no answer. His foot struck something that clattered metallically, and about to pick it up, he halted . . . Was that sound he heard?

He waited, sensing a growing menace, a spine-tingling tension. And abruptly the stone door slid aside and the chamber was flooded with the baleful luminescence.

Blinking in the blinding radiance, Marshall caught sight of Peggy partly within the tomb which had held the remains of Atahualpa—remains now shattered and broken by the impact of her body. Hurled there by the Inca himself!

And Marshall knew why he had suddenly been freed of the demon who had claimed his body.

Gently he extricated the girl from the cavelike opening and stood her on her feet, supporting her weight with one arm, softly calling her name. Her eyes opened, staring blankly—and filling abruptly with stark, wild terror.

"It's all right now, Peggy," Marshall said gently. "Nothing to fear."

She shuddered. "The darkness—that wraith—then your madness, and your striking me—I guess I fainted. Please—get me out of here, Ken before—" She broke off, catching her breath.

"Ken! Marguerite! Hurry—release us!" It was the high-pitched voice of Dr. J. Carlton Ashbery, a voice filled with anxiety, but free of any suggestion of abnormality. Ken saw him now, halfway up the stairs leading to the upper corridor. Beside him crouched the German.

"*Ja!*" Ollendorpf rumbled. "Remove these *verdammte* belts. There iss not much time, for we with our coming haff awakened Viracocha!"

With a shout Ken darted across the room to the stairway, Peggy at his side. He ignored the shambles of shattered bones, crumbling, dust-dry flesh and rotting fabric. Both men themselves again, the Incas dispossessed! With the destruction of the mummies of Apu Tintaya and Huayna Capac, their spirits, like the other wraiths, had been released from Earth, and from the bodies they had claimed.

"Professor," Marshall said fervently, as he unbuckled the belts that held the two men, "this is almost a miracle. We'll get out of this damned place in one piece. And there's enough treasure here to buy Peru!"

"Don't think of treasure now, Kenneth!" Ashbery's voice shook. "Only hurry! We're in greater danger than you can possibly realize. The being who was worshipped by the ancient Chimus and these— undead Incas, lives—and is awake after a sleep of five centuries. Hurry!"

In a moment they were free, whirled to mount the stairway—and suddenly halted!

Halted, all motion arrested. Turned as though hypnotized—moved like four automatons down the steps. Strode mechanically across the chamber of the tombs. Entered the sloping corridor, moved unseeingly into the pulsing flood of cold light . . .

Into Ken Marshall's mind poured alien thoughts, wordless images that somehow seemed to have their origin within his own brain. He saw as in memory the

191

Great God Viracocha seated in glory within an ancient temple. Multitudes bowed before the Lord of all Lords — and it was fitting that they should do so, for he was the Great God whom all men should worship. He would go to Viracocha — would fling himself prostrate before him . . .

Faintly through the web of unnatural ideas, Ken Marshall became aware of the voice of Dr. Ashbery chanting rhythmically in a strange and archaic tongue. Not the Inca — the tongue of the Chimus. Words Marshall could not understand — words of power that swept away the tide of illusion, that freed his mind of alien thoughts. And abruply he realized that he stood at the very edge of the conelike chamber with Peggy, Ashbery and Ollendorpf, facing the veil of light!

As he waited, with Ashbery's chant ringing in his ears, that veil drew aside as a curtain is drawn, and Ken Marshall gazed in awe at — Viracocha!

An image — but this could be no image! It was *alive*, — alive, though a thing of golden yellow metal! Twice the height of a man it towered, the original of the little statuette in Marshall's pocket. The same harpy-curved nose on both, the same cruel, Luciferean expression on a face too large for the squatting bony-limbed body . . . If not a living thing, it was wrought with incredible skill, even to the texture of the golden skin. So marked was the illusion of life that Ken momentarily expected to see it rise and smite them.

The figure squatted on a golden, flat-topped dais, its skeletal limbs drawn up under a bony chin, like the mummies of the Incas. It was framed in the ghastly phosphorescent radiance that filled the room. That radiance emanated from a source behind Viracocha, a pulsing fountain of light pluming up from the floor, brilliant, almost, as a sun, yet cold as radium-glow.

Instantaneous had been Marshall's vision of Viracocha; as he stared, he heard Ashbery's chant mount to a climax, a high-pitched shout of triumph— and on that note it ended. Briefly he wondered at the older man's strange knowledge; knew as the thought formed that the knowledge was a gift of Apu Tintaya, pressed upon his brain cells by the spirit of the Priest. Then speculation was gone in a rush of malevolent words sweeping through his brain.

Words of Viracocha!

"Think you your puny knowledge can save you? You have dared to interfere with the plans of One whose wisdom was old when Earth itself was young! Last of the Elder Race am I—Earthbound by decree of those Elder Ones who passed beyond. Once was I worshiped by all men—and again will men pay homage to Viracocha, Lord of all Lords! Through you were destroyed those whom I purposed to use—and you shall take their place. Bodies you have which I shall claim—minds to do my will—treasure in abundance to lure others of your race to this hidden place. Them also will I claim—and those *they* bring, until my minions shall be without number! Till all men worship the God of Gods!"

Thought seemed to die within the minds of the four. Like robots they stood staring fixedly with unwinking eyes. And there followed that which Ken Marshall afterward told himself could not have happened. Imaginary occurrences implanted in his clutching the image; felt the power of Viracocha's thought arresting the motion. There was alarm in the mental impulse. Was the little image the weapon to pit against its living counterpart?

Again he tried to hurl it, every muscle straining with effort, but his arm was held as though turned to steel. Mentally he writhed in his complete helplessness. Viracocha was dreadfully close.

He heard a hoarse cry almost in his ear: "You protect me, hein?"

The German! Then a flow of Chimu incantation followed in Max Ollendorpf's tones—a powerful grasp wrenched the image from his hand—and the Teuton leaped directly toward the advancing menace! Leaped, his chant unbroken. Swerved, darting around the Viracocha.

It happened too quickly for thought or interference. Marshall caught a momentary glimpse of what seemed to be surprise and confusion upon the metal face—then Ollendorpf was past—hurled himself with the tightly held image into the very heart of the fountain of light!

As one there burst upon the watchers' senses a flare of intense white light and a single scream of insupportable agony—and Max Ollendorpf had disappeared. Gone in an eye-searing flash of glory. For moments the blinding radiance held, centering about the little mass of metal, fusing the gargoyle duplicate of Viracocha. But sight and thought of the little figure were over-shadowed by a greater wonder.

As the little image fused, so fused its monstrous counterpart! Metal dropped from the misshapen head in golden drops like gigantic beads of sweat. An and the others' brains by the evil entity which called itself Viracocha.

Movement within the place where Viracocha sat! New brilliance in the fountain of light, a coldly flaming geyser . . . A tremor running through the golden image . . . It stiffened, crouched—came slowly erect!

Stood motionless, towering mightily above them, a twelve foot monstrosity of shimmering, living gold! Then with ponderous, elephantine slowness, it stepped down from its dais, vibrations reaching them through the rock of the floor . . . Illusion, Ken told himself, desperately. Hypnosis.

He heard Peggy utter a faint, terrified gasp; heard Ollendorpf rasp a guttural Teutonic oath; heard Ashbery's sharp exclamation. And he—he himself was afraid. Terribly afraid! For that incredible monster, that mass of living metal strode lumberingly toward them!

With his pulse hammering wildly in his throat Marshall tried to fall back before the advancing juggernaut. He could not! He did not have to advance, but he could not retreat. And each slow stride brought the thing closer.

Ken's hand groped for his revolver—then he recalled where it was. He touched his useless flashlight, and with one smooth motion he wrenched it from his belt and hurled it at Viracocha. A foot from the image, if image it was, it seemed to meet some invisible barrier; it clattered to the floor.

Desperately Marshall prodded his mind for a way out. His groping hand felt the hard lines of the statuette in his pocket. No weapon. He raised his arm incredible candle it seemed to be, its sharp lines running together, crumbling, sinking in a pool of golden slag. As it sank into formlessness, as its substance sloughed away, the light behind it dimmed — as though its life were bound to the life of Viracocha — as though the radiant fountain, the little image, and Viracocha, the Lord of Lords, were somehow one.

As death crept over the last of the Elder Race, the minds of the paralyzed three were filled with a mad torrent of vituperation. The flood gates of a mental hell seemed to have been hurled aside, freeing an age-long accumulation of absolute evil. Their minds reeled under the impact — reason tottered on its throne — screaming demons of madness clawed at their brains. But even as the last faint flicker of light within the conical room vanished in blackness, and an odor of decay arose from the pool of slag at their feet, the chains of paralysis fell from them, and they fled blindly, heedlessly through the darkness of the corridor.

Somehow they skirted the mountain of wealth in the center of the burial chamber — somehow stumbled up the dust-laden stairs — somehow groped along the upper corridor — up the second stairway to crawl through the opening in the wall.

It seemed almost as though they had been raised from the dead when they stood at last in the safety and sanity of the outer world where a full moon washed the ancient city of Machu Picchu with its clean white light, and a cool wind cleansed their nostrils of the stench of the tomb.

Not a word was spoken as Ken Marshall led the way

to the tethered pack animals, and by the light of the moon prepared for travel. Many miles must be placed between them and this city of dread before speech could bear the burden of their thoughts. All of them, Marshall knew, were thinking of the last heroic gesture of quarrelsome Max Ollendorpf—and of that monstrous entity which might even yet be lurking, a disembodied specter, in the black shadows of that unhallowed chamber.

The Doom Chant of
Than-Kul
By Robert E. Howard

The Doom Chant of Than-Kul

Atlantis lies in the cold jade sea
Where the sea-ghosts' swords flame endlessly—
Flame, flame!
And spectres know
How Zalthas came
With the kite and crow—
How Zalthas came and the ocean's flow
Ran coiling red in the long ago.
Green in trough,
White on the crest.
Sea-kings oft
Sank here to rest.
When the blood-red sun sank dimming,
When the stars in the night were ghostly white,
The snake of the sea came swimming.
Rise through the dusky emerald surge,
Through the glimmering fathoms, strange and deep,
Till the ocean-jade and the sky-jade merge;
There you will find Than-kul asleep.
Rock, red boat, on the sapphire tide—
Than-kul has burst the bars.

He found no sea-love until he died,
In the silence of the stars.
Over the deeps come eerily
The whispering breezes of the sea.

—Robert E. Howard

Save The Children
By Steve Rasnic Tem

There are some nightmares you don't wake up from.

Save The Children!

by Steve Rasnic Tem

He awoke with a start, the soft, measured voice still present in his thoughts. *Think of the children*, it repeated. *Please save them.*

Half asleep he rose up on his elbows, turned to Margaret's still form beside him, and groggily said, "Let's go now; let's save them," and after a brief pause, "Think of the children. They're in danger."

"Whaaa?" She blinked her eyes, then stared at him. "Oh, Michael. Not *again.*"

"Please save them." He looked at her through half-closed eyes.

She sat up in bed and gingerly poked his shoulder. "You're still asleep, Michael. You just have to stop this. Every morning now."

He closed his eyes completely, fluttered the lids, then opened them. "Nothing . . . nothing. I guess I was dreaming."

Michael lay back onto the pillow and stared at the ceiling, realizing it had been his own voice speaking in the dream.

He shaved slowly that morning, mulling over his advertising campaign for Smith and Reynolds Toy. He had been trying to develop a tie-in between the new Commander Dick Action Doll and the rest of the S & R line of war toys. He'd been brooding over the problem all week; the presentations were close, but he felt there was something missing. The sales copy just wasn't coming together.

Think of the children. A few seconds passed before he realized he was hearing that gentle, lulling voice, his own voice, again. *They're screaming for our help.*

Suddenly Michael felt half-asleep again, and it was hard to think.

Please save the children. You can leave now. They're jamming the city. They're crowded into the subway station; they're stacked into the auditorium like wood.

Margaret was staring at him from the bathroom doorway. "What are you doing?"

Michael just looked at her.

"Is something the matter, Michael?" Her lips were pursed.

He looked at her awhile, barely recognizing her, then realized she must have been talking to him. "Guess I'd better hurry . . . I don't want to be late . . ."

Hurry. The children need your help.

"Maybe you should call in sick today. You don't look well, Michael."

"No . . . I have to get into town. I need to hurry."

Margaret shook her head doubtfully, then left.

The sky was beginning to cloud over as he drove to work. By the time he arrived at the office a fine mist had begun to fall. Very few people seemed to be about, which was odd. Two children, one holding a rose, the other a baseball glove, stared at him as he entered the building.

"You're late, Michael," his boss told him flatly as he walked into the presentation room.

Jackson, one of the other partners in the firm, and a coworker on the S & R account gestured a vague greeting as Michael took his chair before a large table covered with toys, models, and simulated desert and mountainous terrain.

"Got something for you to see, Michael," Jackson stood and walked to a side door. He opened it, motioned with his forefinger to someone in the other room.

A small boy, perhaps five or six, came through the door. He wore ankle-length blue trousers with suspenders, a yellow and red-striped polo shirt. The child looked as if he had walked out of a Norman Rockwell painting: red-haired, blue-eyed, skinny.

The boy stared at Michael. Michael looked away.

Commander Dick jumped out of the green jeep awkwardly, with one gigantic, stiff-legged hop. He dived into a shallow foxhole just as the jeep exploded into a shower of plastic fragments.

Another jeep rammed a large tank, both exploding into a profusion of plastic parts. Commander Dick staggered up, hopped around with one leg missing. A narrow yellow tube snaked out of the bottom of his back, around irregularities in the paper mache terrain, and up into the control box the small boy was gripping with strained, white-knuckled hands. He stared at the game board vacantly, a half-smile playing with his lips.

"So . . . what do you think?" Michael suddenly realized that Jackson was standing over him.

Go down into the city. You can save them now.

Michael could just stare at Jackson, his head and neck rigid with tension.

"Michael? Something wrong?"

Hurry. The children need your help.

"Oh . . . oh, sorry. It's fine . . . fine. Good idea."

Don't be late. Go down and find them where they've been hid.

"Thought you'd like it," Jackson chuckled, then ushered the small boy out the door.

Michael left work early, claiming illness. There seemed to be no one on the streets as he made his way home.

Why should I react that way? he thought. *Why am I so paranoid? It can't be the war toys; kids just imitate what they see. Never bothered me before.* He almost chuckled, not sure why, but the toy demonstration accompanied by these obsessive pleadings . . . it just seemed too much, bathetic, almost ludicrous to him.

They're crowded into the subway station; they're stacked into the auditorium like wood.

Children were beginning to line the streets in twos and threes.

Please save them.

Children were walking out in front of his car. He had to swerve desperately to avoid them.

The children are screaming. They've no mothers or fathers.

Children were pushing and shoving, trampling each other in their attempts to reach his car, to be struck by his car.

Don't let them down. They're packed into every corner in the town.

Michael suddenly realized he was screaming.

He awoke with a start. Again. He thought he was hearing the soft, measured voice again, but it was his wife speaking from her side of the bed.

"You have to stop this, Michael. I haven't been able to sleep with all your craziness."

"The children . . ."

"Is it because of the baby, Michael? I was disappointed too; I wanted kids. Do you feel guilty, Michael? Is that what all this is about? Or is it me that you hate?"

"They won't leave me alone . . ." He was gripping her arm.

"Michael . . . *nothing* could be done . . . *Michael.* This *has* to *stop!*"

He was awake again. He didn't know how long. His wife's form seemed soft and peaceful, her face white in the moonlight.

Half-asleep. Thinking seemed difficult.

He thought he had heard screaming, but knew it couldn't be.

He wanted to go into the town, but wasn't sure why.

Michael walked into the bathroom, shaved, and dressed in his sharkskin suit. Then he pulled it off. He wore his golf togs into the kitchen, got a glass of milk. Then he ripped them off.

He shaved again, and then he shaved once more.

"Their teeth are rotting. They're growing larger, becoming older every day," he muttered to himself. "I have to reach them in time."

Michael suddenly realized he was lying on the bathroom floor, clothes strewn about. "If I hurry I'll make it."

Michael pulled himself off the floor, slipped into his work clothes hanging in a small closet off the shower, then put on his tennis shoes. Then he lay down again. "I'll get dressed right away. I'll do the best I can."

Michael got up off the floor and took off his clothes. "If I hurry now . . ."

Michael shaved for the ninth time that evening. His face was scratched and bleeding.

He could hear them screaming, the screams getting louder all the time. He staggered over to the bathroom window, wondering if he could see them from there, imagining them jamming the suburbs, crowding the ditchlines, packed into the bushes and trees.

"I'm going to hurry; I'm going to save you all," he whispered into the darkness as he tied his broad red tie around his bare, collarless neck.

He would hurry. He would waste no time. He would dress in his finest clothes and soon he would save them. Soon he would be running down the city streets, seeking them out.

* * *

He descended the staircase to the ground floor, half-awake, half-dreaming of napalmed children, battered babies, little boys with amputated legs, little girls raped and beaten.

He staggered past the open window, his loose bathrobe and tie fluttering in the breeze. He turned and leaned into the cellar door, opened that, and descended.

Michael took each step gingerly, wondered what his own child might have been like, if he could have saved him. He remembered the fear he felt when she told him of the pregnancy, the fear he wasn't capable of taking care of a child.

He stood at the bottom of the staircase, watching the darkness ebb and flow around him. But wasn't there only so much one man could do?

There were soft sighings in the darkness.

. . . save us . . . please, save us . . .

He couldn't protect himself as a child. His father could still strike out at him, torture him, and there was nothing he could do . . .

Think of us . . .

Like the rustlings of dead leaves they touched him, softly at first, over his entire body. Then harder as the children congealed into one hand, stroke, arm, one gross misshapen baby's form. Harder still as he began to cry, and they, comforting him, stroked too hard, until he cried out from the pain.

Again, he could hear their cries, the soft measured crying voice his own.

The Sea Gods
By Clark Ashton Smith

The Sea-Gods

Beneath the sunset and the sea
Their coral-builded cities be;
They keep an old forgotten reign,
A purple, far supremacy.

The azure-girdled suns that roam,
And moons that tread the silvering foam,
Are vague above their ocean-vales;
And shaken dawns their evenings dome.

Their eyes like changing emeralds gleam
Through gulfs where winy twilights stream;
And with blue weeds their tresses flow,
As in a dark, confused dream.

But often, when long afterglows
In cold and spectral evening close,
On lonely seas they rise, and cry
From foam left grey by sunset's rose.

Or in the mystic waves and wan,
Hushed by the moon's marmoreal dawn,
They moan as moans the muted surf
On shores of windless isles withdrawn.

Known to their dim supremacy
The deep's forgotten secrets be;
Their old, eternal vestures are
The purples of the flowing sea.

—Clark Ashton Smith

Ooze
By Anthony M. Rud

Ooze

by Anthony M. Rud

In the heart of a second-growth piney-woods jungle of southern Alabama, a region sparsely settled by back-woods blacks and Cajans—that queer, half-wild people descended from Acadian exiles of the middle eighteenth century—stands a strange, enormous ruin.

Interminable trailers of Cherokee rose, white-laden during a single month of spring, have climbed the heights of its three remaining walls. Palmetto fans rise knee high above the base. A dozen scattered live oaks, now belying their nomenclature because of choking tufts of gray, Spanish moss and two-foot circlets of mistletoe parasite which have stripped bare of foliage the gnarled, knotted limbs, lean fantastic beards against the crumbling brick.

Immediately beyond, where the ground becomes soggier and lower—dropping away hopelessly into the tangle of dogwood, holly, poison sumac and pitcher plants that is Moccasin Swamp—undergrowth of ti-ti and annis has formed a protecting wall impenetrable to all save the furtive ones. Some few outcasts utilize the stinking depths of that sinister swamp, distilling "shinny" of "pure cawn" liquor for illicit trade.

Tradition states that this is the case, at least—a tradition which antedates that of the premature ruin by many decades. I believe it, for during evenings intervening between investigations of the awesome spot I often was approached as a possible customer by wood-billies who could not fathom how anyone dared venture near without plenteous fortification of liquid courage.

I knew "shinny," therefore I did not purchase it for personal consumption. A dozen times I bought a quart or two, merely to establish credit among the Cajans, pouring away the vile stuff immediately into the sodden ground. It seemed then that only through filtration and condensation of their dozens of weird tales regarding "Daid House" could I arrive at understanding of the mystery and weight of horror hanging about the place.

Certain it is that out of all the superstitious cautioning, head-wagging and whispered nonsensities I obtained only two indisputable facts. The first was that no money, and no supporting battery of ten-gauge shotguns loaded with chilled shot, could induce either Cajan or darky of the region to approach within five hundred yards of that flowering wall! The second fact I shall dwell upon later.

Perhaps it would be as well, as I am only a mouth-piece in this chronicle, to relate in brief why I came to Alabama on this mission.

I am a scribbler of general fact articles, no fiction

writer as was Lee Cranmer—though doubtless the confession is superfluous. Lee was my roommate during college days. I knew his family well, admiring John Corliss Cranmer even more than I admired the son and friend—and almost as much as Peggy Breede whom Lee married. Peggy liked me, but that was all. I cherish sanctified memory of her for just that much, as no other woman before or since has granted this gangling dyspeptic even a hint of joyous and sorrowful intimacy.

Work kept me to the city. Lee, on the other hand, coming of wealthy family—and, from the first, earning from his short-stories and novel royalties more than I wrested from editorial coffers—needed no anchorage. He and Peggy honeymooned a four-month trip to Alaska, visited Honolulu next winter, fished for salmon on Cain's River, New Brunswick, and generally enjoyed the outdoors at all seasons.

They kept an apartment in Wilmette, near Chicago, yet, during the few spring and fall seasons they were "home," both preferred to rent a suite at one of the country clubs to which Lee belonged. I suppose they spent thrice or five times the amount Lee actually earned, yet for my part I only honored that the two should find such great happiness in life and still accomplish artistic triumph.

They were honest, zestful young Americans, the type—and pretty nearly the *only* type—two million dollars cannot spoil. John Corliss Cranmer, father of Lee, though as different from his boy as a microscope is different from a painting by Remington, was even further from being dollar conscious. He lived in a world bounded only by the widening horizon of biological science—and his love for the two who would carry on

221

that Cranmer name.

Many a time I used to wonder how it could be that as gentle, clean-souled and lovable a gentleman as John Corliss Cranmer could have ventured so far into scientific research without attaining small-caliber atheism. Few do. He believed both in God and human kind. To accuse him of murdering his boy and the girl wife who had come to be loved as the mother of baby Elsie — as well as blood and flesh of his own family — was a gruesome, terrible absurdity! Yes, even when John Corliss Cranmer was declared unmistakably insane!

Lacking a relative in the world, baby Elsie was given to me — and the middle-aged couple who had accompanied the three as servants about half of the known world. Elsie would be Peggy over again. I worshiped her, knowing that if my stewardship of her interests could make of her a woman of Peggy's loveliness and worth I should not have lived in vain. And at four Elsie stretched out her arms to me after a vain attempt to jerk out the bobbed tail of Lord Dick, my tolerant old Airedale — and called me "papa."

I felt a deep-down choking . . . yes, those strangely long black lashes some day might droop in fun or coquetry, but now baby Elsie held a wistful, trusting seriousness in depths of ultramarine eyes — that same seriousness which only Lee had brought to Peggy.

Responsibility in one instant became double. That she might come to love me as more than foster parent was my dearest wish. Still, through selfishness I could not rob her of rightful heritage; she must know in after years. And the tale that I would tell her must not be the horrible suspicion which had been bandied about in common talk!

I went to Alabama, leaving Elsie in the competent hands of Mrs. Daniels and her husband, who had helped care for her since birth.

In my possession, prior to the trip, were the scant facts known to authorities at the time of John Corliss Cranmer's escape and disappearance. They were incredible enough.

For conducting biological research upon forms of protozon life, John Corliss Cranmer had hit upon this region of Alabama. Near a great swamp teeming with microscopic organisms, and situated in a semitropical belt where freezing weather rarely intruded to harden the bogs, the spot seemed ideal for his purpose.

Through Mobile he could secure supplies daily by truck. The isolation suited. With only an octoroon man to act as chef, house man and valet for the times he entertained no visitors, he brought down scientific apparatus, occupying temporary quarters in the village of Burdett's Corners while his woods house was in process of construction.

By all accounts the Lodge, as he termed it, was a substantial affair of eight or nine rooms, built of logs and planed lumber bought at Oak Grove. Lee and Peggy were expected to spend a portion of each year with him; quail, wild turkey and deer abounded, which fact made such a vacation certain to please the pair. At other times all save four rooms was closed.

This was in 1907, the year of Lee's marriage. Six years later when I came down, no sign of a house remained except certain mangled and rotting timbers projecting from viscid soil — or what seemed like soil. And a twelve-foot wall of brick had been built to enclose the house completely! One portion of this had fallen *inward!*

II

I wasted weeks of time at first, interviewing officials of
the police department at Mobile, the town marshals
and county sheriffs of Washington and Mobile
counties, and officials of the psychopathic hospital from
which Cranmer made his escape.

In substance the story was one of baseless homicidal
mania. Cranmer the elder had been away until late fall,
attending two scientific conferences in the North, and
then going abroad to compare certain of his findings
with those of a Dr. Gemmler of Prague University.
Unfortunately, Gemmler was assassinated by a religious
fanatic shortly afterward. The fanatic voiced virulent
objection to all Mendelian research as blasphemous.
This was his only defense. He was hanged.

Search of Gemmler's notes and effects revealed
nothing save an immense amount of laboratory data on
karyokinesis — the process of chromosome arrangement
occurring in first growing cells of higher animal
embryos. Apparently Cranmer had hoped to develop
some similarities, or point out differences between
hereditary factors occurring in lower forms of life and
those half-demonstrated in the cat and monkey. The
authorities had found nothing that helped me.
Cranmer had gone crazy; was that not sufficient
explanation?

Perhaps it was for them, but not for me — and Elsie.

But to the slim basis of fact I was able to unearth:

No one wondered when a fortnight passed without
appearance of any person from the Lodge. Why should
anyone worry? A provision salesman in Mobile called up

twice, but failed to complete a connection. He merely shrugged. The Cranmers had gone away somewhere on a trip. In a week, a month, a year they would be back. Meanwhile he lost commissions, but what of it? He had no responsibility for these queer nuts up there in the piney-woods. Crazy? Of course! Why should any guy with millions to spend shut himself up among the Cajans and draw microscope-enlarged notebook pictures of—what the saleman called—"germs"?

A stir was aroused at the end of the fortnight, but the commotion confined itself to building circles. Twenty carloads of building brick, fifty bricklayers, and a quarteracre of fine-meshed wire—the sort used for screening off pens of rodents and small marsupials in a zoological garden—were ordered, *damn expense, hurry!* by an unshaved, tattered man who identified himself with difficulty as John Corliss Cranmer.

He looked strange, even then. A certified check for the total amount, given in advance, and another check of absurd size slung toward a labor *entrepreneur*, silenced objection, however. These millionaires were apt to be flighty. When they wanted something they wanted it at tap of the bell. Well, why not drag down the big profits? A poorer man would have been jacked up in a day. Cranmer's fluid gold bathed him in immunity to criticism.

The encircling wall was built, and roofed with wire netting which drooped about the squat-pitch of the Lodge. Curious inquiries of workmen went unanswered until the final day.

Then Cranmer, a strange, intense apparition who showed himself more shabby than a quay derelict, assembled every man jack of the workmen. In one hand

225

he grasped a wad of blue slips—fifty-six of them. In the other he held a Luger automatic.

"I offer each man a thousand dollars for *silence!*" he announced. "As an alternative—*death!* You know little. Will all of you consent to swear upon your honor that nothing which has occurred here will be mentioned elsewhere? By this I mean *absolute* silence! You will not come back here to investigate anything. You will not tell your wives. You will not open your mouths even upon the witness stand in case you are called! My price is one thousand apiece.

"In case one of you betrays me *I give you my word that this man shall die!* I am rich. I can hire men to do murder. Well, what do you say?"

The men glanced apprehensively about. The threatening Luger decided them. To a man they accepted the blue slips—and, save for one witness who lost all sense of fear and morality in drink, none of the fifty-six has broken his pledge, as far as I know. That one bricklayer died later in delirium tremens.

It might have been different had not John Corliss Cranmer escaped.

III

They found him the first time, mouthing meaningless phrases concerning an amoeba—one of the tiny forms of protoplasmic life he was known to have studied. Also he leaped into a hysteria of self-accusation. He had murdered two innocent people! The tragedy was his crime. He had drowned them in ooze! Ah, God!

Unfortunately for all concerned, Cranmer, dazed and indubitably stark insane, chose to perform a strange travesty on fishing four miles to the west of his lodge—on the further border of Moccasin Swamp. His clothing had been torn to shreds, his hat was gone, and he was coated from head to foot with gluey mire. It was far from strange that the good folk of Shanksville, who never had glimpsed the eccentric millionaire, failed to associate him with Cranmer.

They took him in, searched his pockets—finding no sign save an inordinate sum of money—and then put him under medical care. Two precious weeks elapsed before Dr. Quirk reluctantly acknowledged that he could do nothing more for this patient, and notified the proper authorities.

Then much more time was wasted. Hot April and half of still hotter May passed by before the loose ends were connected. Then it did little good to know that this raving unfortunate was Cranmer, or that the two persons of whom he shouted in disconnected delirium actually had disappeared. Alienists absolved him of responsibility. He was confined in a cell reserved for the violent.

Meanwhile, strange things occurred back at the Lodge—which now, for good and sufficient reason, was becoming known to dwellers of the woods as Dead House. Until one of the walls fell in, however, there had been no chance to see—unless one possessed the temerity to climb either one of the tall live oaks, or mount the barrier itself. No doors or opening of any sort had been placed in that hastily-constructed wall!

By the time the western side of the wall fell, not a native for miles around but feared the spot far more than even the bottomless, snake-infested bogs which lay to west and north.

The single statement was all John Corliss Cranmer ever gave to the world. It proved sufficient. An immediate search was instituted. It showed that less than three weeks before the day of initial reckoning, his son and Peggy had come to visit him for the second time that winter—leaving Elsie behind in company of the Daniels pair. They had rented a pair of Gordons for quail hunting, and had gone out. That was the last anyone had seen of them.

The backwoods Negro who glimpsed them stalking a covey behind their two pointing dogs had known no more—even when sweated through twelve hours of third degree. Certain suspicious circumstances (having to do only with his regular pursuit of "shinny" transportation) had caused him to fall under suspicion at first. He was dropped.

Two days later the scientist himself was apprehended—a gibbering idiot who sloughed his pole—holding on to the baited hook—into a marsh where nothing save moccasins, an errant alligator, or amphibian life could have been snared.

His mind was three-quarters dead. Cranmer then was in the state of the dope fiend who rouses to a sitting position to ask seriously how many Bolshevists were killed by Julius Caesar before he was stabbed by Brutus, or why it was that Roller canaries sang only on Wednesday evenings. He knew that tragedy of the most sinister sort had stalked through his life—but little more, at first.

Later the police obtained that one statement that he had murdered two human beings, but never could means or motive be established. Official guess as to the means was no more than wild conjecture; it mentioned

228

enticing the victims to the noisome depths of Moccasin Swamp, there to let them flounder and sink.

The two were his son and daughter-in-law, Lee and Peggy!

IV

By feigning coma — then awakening with suddenness to assault three attendants with incredible ferocity and strength — John Corliss Cranmer escaped from Elizabeth Ritter Hospital.

How he hid, how he managed to traverse sixty-odd intervening miles and still balk detection, remains a minor mystery to be explained only by the assumption that maniacal cunning sufficed to outwit saner intellects.

Traverse these miles he did, though until I was fortunate enough to uncover evidence to this effect, it was supposed generally that he had made his escape as stowaway on one of the banana boats, or had buried himself in some portion of the nearer woods where he was unknown. The truth ought to be welcome to householders of Shanksville, Burdett's Corners and vicinage — those excusably prudent ones who to this day keep loaded shotguns handy and barricade their doors at nightfall.

The first ten days of my investigation may be touched upon in brief. I made headquarters in Burdett's Corners, and drove out each morning, carrying lunch and returning for my grits and pineywoods pork or mutton before nightfall. My first plan had been to camp out at the edge of the swamp, for opportunity to enjoy the outdoors comes rarely in my direction. Yet after one cursory examination of the premises, I abandoned the idea. I did not *want* to camp alone there. And I am less superstitious than a real estate agent.

It was, perhaps, psychic warning; more probably the queer, faint, salty odor as of fish left to decay, which hung about the ruin, made too unpleasant an impression upon my olfactory sense. I experienced a distinct chill every time the lengthening shadows caught me near Dead House.

The smell impressed me. In newspaper reports of the case one ingenious explanation had been worked out. To the rear of the spot where Dead House had stood—inside the wall—was a swampy hollow circular in shape. Only a little real mud lay in the bottom of the bowllike depression now, but one reporter on the staff of *The Mobile Register* guessed that during the tenancy of the lodge it had been a fishpool. Drying up of the water had killed the fish, who now permeated the remnant of mud with this foul odor.

The possibility that Cranmer had needed to keep fresh fish at hand for some of his experiments silenced the natural objection that in a country where every stream holds gar pike, bass, catfish and many other edible varieties, no one would dream of stocking a stagnant puddle.

After tramping about the enclosure, testing the queerly brittle, desiccated top stratum of earth within and speculating concerning the possible purpose of the wall, I cut off a long limb of chinaberry and probed the mud. One fragment of fish spine would confirm the guess of that imaginative reporter.

I found nothing resembling a piscal skeleton, but

established several facts. First, this mud crater had definite bottom only three or four feet below the surface of remaining ooze. Second, the fishy stench became stronger as I stirred. Third, at one time the mud, water, or whatever had comprised the balance of content, had reached the rim of the bowl. The last showed by certain marks plain enough when the crusty, two-inch stratum of upper coating was broken away. It was puzzling.

The nature of that thin, desiccated effluvium which seemed to cover everything even to the lower foot or two of brick, came in for next inspection. It was strange stuff, unlike any earth I ever had seen, though undoubtedly some form of scum drained in from the swamp at the time of river floods or cloudbursts (which in this section are common enough in spring and fall). It crumbled beneath the fingers. When I walked over it, the stuff crunched hollowly. In fainter degree it possessed the fishy odor also.

I took some samples where it lay thickest upon the ground, and also a few where there seemed to be no more than a depth of a sheet of paper. Later I would have a laboratory analysis made.

Apart from any possible bearing the stuff might have upon the disappearance of my three friends, I felt the tug of article interest—that wonder over anything strange or seemingly inexplicable which lends the hunt for fact a certain glamor and romance all its own. To myself I was going to have to explain sooner or later just why this layer covered the entire space within the walls and was not perceptible *anywhere* outside! The enigma could wait, however—or so I decided.

Far more interesting were the traces of violence apparent on wall and what once had been a house. The latter seemed to have been ripped from its foundations by a giant hand, crushed out of semblance to a dwelling, and then cast in fragments about the base of wall—mainly on the south side, where heaps of twisted, broken timbers lay in profusion. On the opposite side there had been such heaps once, but now only charred sticks, coated with that gray-black, omipresent coat of desiccation, remained. These piles of charcoal had been sifted and examined most carefully by the authorities, as one theory had been advanced that Cranmer had burned the bodies of his victims. Yet no sign whatever of human remains was discovered.

The fire, however, pointed out one odd fact which controverted the reconstructions made by detectives months before. The latter, suggesting the dried scum to have drained in from the swamp, believed that the house timbers had floated out to the sides of the wall—there to arrange themselves in a series of piles! The absurdity of such a theory showed even more plainly in the fact that *if* the scum had filtered through in such a flood, the timbers most certainly had been dragged into piles *previously!* Some had burned—*and the scum coated their charred surfaces!*

What had been the force which had torn the lodge to bits as if in spiteful fury? Why had the parts of the wreckage been burned, the rest to escape?

Right here I felt was the keynote to the mystery, yet I could imagine no explanation. That John Corliss Cranmer himself—physically sound, yet a man who for decades had led a sedentary life—could have accomplished such destruction, unaided, was difficult to believe.

V

I turned my attention to the wall, hoping for evidence which might suggest another theory.

That wall had been an example of the worst snide construction. Though little more than a year old, the parts left standing showed evidence that they had begun to decay the day the last brick was laid. The mortar had fallen from the interstices. Here and there a brick had cracked and dropped out. Fibrils of the climbing vines had penetrated crevices, working for early destruction.

And one side already had fallen.

It was here that the first glimmering suspicion of the terrible truth was forced upon me. The scattered bricks, even those which had rolled inward toward the gaping foundation lodge, *had not been coated with scum!* This was curious, yet it could be explained by surmise that the flood itself had undermined this weakest portion of the wall. I cleared away a mass of brick from the spot on which the structure had stood; to my surprise I found it exceptionally firm! Hard red clay lay beneath! The flood conception was faulty; only some great force, exerted from inside or outside, could have wreaked such destruction.

When careful measurement, analysis and deduction convinced me — mainly from the fact that the lowermost layers of brick all had fallen *outward*, while the upper portions toppled *in* — I began to link up this mysterious and horrific force with the one which had rent the Lodge asunder. It looked as though a typhoon or gigantic centrifuge had needed elbow room in ripping down the wooden structure.

But I got nowhere with the theory, though in

ordinary affairs I am called a man of too great imaginative tendencies. No less than three editors have cautioned me on this point. Perhaps it was the narrowing influence of great personal sympathy—yes, and love. I make no excuses, though beyond a dim understanding that some terrific, implacable force must have made this spot his playground, I ended my ninth day of note-taking and investigation almost as much in the dark as I had been while a thousand miles away in Chicago.

Then I started among the darkies and Cajans. A whole day I listened to yarns of the days which preceded Cranmer's escape from Elizabeth Ritter Hospital—days in which furtive men sniffed poisoned air for miles around Dead House, finding the odor intolerable. Days in which it seemed none possessed nerve enough to approach close. Days when the most fanciful tales of medieval superstitions were spun. These tales I shall not give; the truth is incredible enough.

At noon upon the eleventh day I chanced upon Rori Pailleron, a Cajan—and one of the least prepossessing of all with whom I had come in contact. "Chanced" perhaps is a bad word. I had listed every dweller of the woods within a five mile radius. Rori was sixteenth on my list. I went to him only after interviewing all four of the Crabiers and two whole families of Pichons. And Rori regarded me with the utmost suspicion until I made him a present of the two quarts of "shinny" purchased of the Pichons.

Because long practice has perfected me in the technique of seeming to drink another man's awful liquor—no, I'm not an absolute prohibitionist; fine wine or twelve-year-in-cask Bourbon whiskey arouses my definite interest — I fooled Pailleron from the start. I shall omit preliminaries, and leap to the first admission from him that he knew more concerning Dead House and its former inmates than any of the other darkies or Cajans roundabout.

". . . But I ain't talkin'. *Sacre!* If I should open my gab, what might fly out? It is for keeping silent, y'r damn right! . . ."

I agreed. He was a wise man — educated to some extent in the queer schools and churches maintained exclusively by Cajans in the depths of the woods, yet naive withal.

We drank. And I never had to ask another leading question. The liquor made him want to interest me; and the only extraordinary topic in this whole neck of the woods was the Dead House.

Three-quarters of a pint of acrid, nauseous fluid, and he hinted darkly. A pint, and he told me something I scarcely could believe. Another half-pint. . . . But I shall give his confession in condensed form.

He had known Joe Sibley, the octoroon chef, house-man and valet who served Cranmer. Through Joe, Rori had furnished certain indispensables in way of food to the Cranmer household. At first, these salable articles had been exclusively vegetable — white and yellow turnip, sweet potatoes, corn and beans — but later, *meat!*

Yes, meat especially — whole lambs, slaughtered and quartered, the coarsest variety of piney-woods pork and beef, all in immense quantity!

VI

In December of the fatal winter Lee and his wife stopped down at the Lodge for ten days or thereabouts.

They were enroute to Cuba at the time, intending to be away five or six weeks. Their original plan had been only to wait over a day or so in the piney-woods, but something caused an amendment to the scheme.

The two dallied. Lee seemed to have become vastly absorbed in something—so much absorbed that it was only when Peggy insisted upon continuing their trip that he could tear himself away.

It was during those ten days that he began buying meat. Meager bits of it at first—a rabbit, a pair of squirrels, or perhaps a few quail beyond the number he and Peggy shot. Rori furnished the game, thinking nothing of it except that Lee paid double prices—and insisted upon keeping the purchases secret from other members of the household.

"I'm putting it across on the Governor, Rori!" he said once with a wink. "Going to give him the shock of his life. So you mustn't let on, even to Joe about what I want you to do. Maybe it won't work out, but if it does . . .! Dad'll have the scientific world at his feet! He doesn't blow his own horn anywhere near enough, you know."

Rori didn't know. Hadn't a suspicion what Lee was talking about. Still, if this rich, young idiot wanted to pay him a half dollar in good silver coin for a quail that anyone—himself included—could knock down with a five-cent shell, Rori was well satisfied to keep his mouth shut. Each evening he brought some of the small game. And each day Lee Cranmer seemed to have use for an additional quail or so. . . .

When he was ready to leave for Cuba, Lee came forward with the strangest of propositions. He fairly whispered his vehemence and desire for secrecy! He would tell Rori, and would pay the Cajan five hundred dollars—half in advance, and half at the end of five weeks when Lee himself would return from Cuba—provided Rori agreed to adhere absolutely to a certain secret program! The money was more than a fortune to Rori; it was undreamt-of affluence. The Cajan acceded.

"He wuz tellin' me then how the ol' man had raised some kind of pet," Rori confided, "an' wanted to get shet of it. So he give it to Lee, tellin' him to kill it, but Lee was sot on foolin' him. W'at I ask yer is, w'at kind of a pet is it w'at lives down in a mud sink an' *eats a couple hawgs every night?*"

I couldn't imagine, so I pressed him for further details. Here at last was something which sounded like a clue!

He really knew too little. The agreement with Lee provided that if Rori carried out the provisions exactly, he should be paid extra and at his exorbitant scale of all additional outlay, when Lee returned.

The young man gave him a daily schedule which Rori showed. Each evening he was to procure, slaughter and cut up a definite—and growing—amount of meat. Every item was checked, and I saw that they ran from five pounds up to *forty!*

"What in heaven's name, did you do with it?" I demanded, excited now and pouring him an additional drink for fear caution might return to him.

"Took it through the bushes in back an' slung it in the mud sink there! An' suthin' come up an' drug it down!"

"A 'gator?"

"*Diable!* How should I know? It was dark. I wouldn't go close." He shuddered, and the fingers which lifted his glass shook as with sudden chill. "Mebbe you'd of done it, huh? Not *me,* though! The young fellah tole me to sling it in, an' I slung it.

"A couple times I come around in the light, but there wasn't nuthin' there you could see. Jes' mud, an' some water. Mebbe the thing didn't come out in day-times. . . ."

"Perhaps not," I agreed, straining every mental resource to imagine what Lee's sinister pet could have been. "But you said something about *two hogs a day?* What did you mean by that? This paper, proof enough that you're telling the truth so far, states that on the thirty-fifth day you were to throw forty pounds of meat—any kind—into the sink. Two hogs, even the piney-woods variety, weigh a lot more than forty pounds!"

"Them was after—after he come back!"

From this point onward, Rori's tale became more and more enmeshed in the vagaries induced by bad liquor. His tongue thickened. I shall give his story without attempt to reproduce further verbal barbarities, or the occasional prodding I had to give in order to keep him from maundering into foolish jargon.

Lee had paid munificently. His only objection to the manner in which Rori had carried out his orders was that the orders themselves had been deficient. The pet, he said had grown enormously. It was hungry, ravenous. Lee himself had supplemented the fare with huge pails of scraps from the kitchen.

From that day Lee purchased from Rori whole sheep

and hogs! The Cajan continued to bring the carcasses at nightfall, but no longer did Lee permit him to approach the pool. The young man appeared chronically excited now. He had a tremendous secret—one the extent of which even his father did not guess, and one which would astonish the world! Only a week or two more and he would spring it. First he would have to arrange certain data.

Then came the day when everyone disappeared from Dead House. Rori came around several times, but concluded that all of the occupants had folded tents and departed—doubtless taking their mysterious "pet" along. Only when he saw from a distance Joe, the octoroon servant, returning along the road on foot toward the Lodge, did his slow mental processes begin to ferment. That afternoon Rori visited the strange place for the next to last time.

He did not go to the Lodge itself—and there were reasons. While still some hundreds of yards away from the place a terrible, sustained screaming reached his ears! It was faint, yet unmistakably the voice of Joe! Throwing a pair of number two shells into the breech of his shotgun, Rori hurried on, taking his usual path through the brush at the back.

He saw—and as he told me even "shinny" drunkenness fled his chattering tones—Joe, the octoroon. Aye, he stood in the yard, far from the pool into which Rori had thrown the carcasses—*and Joe could not move!*

Rori failed to explain in full, but *something*, a slimy, amorphous something, which glistened in the sunlight, already engulfed the man to his shoulders! Breath was cut off. Joe's contorted face writhed with horror and beginning suffocation. One hand—all that was free of the rest of him!—beat feebly upon the rubbery, translucent thing that was engulfing his body!

Then Joe sank from sight. . . .

VII

Five days of liquored indulgence passed before Rori, alone in his shaky cabin, convinced himself that he had seen a phantasy born of alcohol. He came back the last time—to find a high wall of brick surrounding the Lodge, and including the pool of mud into which he had thrown the meat!

While he hesitated, circling the place without discovering an opening—which he would not have dared to use, even had he found it—a crashing, tearing of timbers, and persistent sound of awesome destruction came from within. He swung himself into one of the oaks near the wall. And he was just in time to see the last supporting stanchions of the Lodge give way *outward!*

The whole structure came apart. The roof fell in—yet seemed to move after it had fallen! Logs of wall deserted retaining grasp of their spikes like layers of plywood in the grasp of the shearing machine!

That was all. Soddenly intoxicated now, Rori mumbled more phrases, giving me the idea that on another day when he became sober once more, he might add to his statements, but I—numbed to the soul—scarcely cared. If that which he related was true, what nightmare of madness must have been consummated here!

I could vision some things now which concerned Lee and Peggy, horrible things. Only remembrance of Elsie kept me faced forward in the search—for now it seemed almost that the handiwork of a madman must be preferred to what Rori claimed to have seen! What had been that sinister, translucent thing? That glistening thing which jumped upward about a man, smothering, engulfing?

Queerly enough, though such a theory as came most easily to mind now would have outraged reason in me if suggested concerning total strangers, I asked myself only what details of Rori's revelation had been exaggerated by fright and fumes of liquor. And as I sat on the creaking bench in his cabin, staring unseeing as he lurched down to the floor, fumbling with a lock box of green tin which lay under his cot, and muttering, the answer to all my questions lay within reach!

It was not until next day, however, that I made the discovery. Heavy of heart I had reexamined the spot where the Lodge had stood, then made my way to the Cajan's cabin again, seeking sober confirmation of what he had told me during intoxication.

In imagining that such a spree for Rori would be ended by a single night, however, I was mistaken. He lay sprawled almost as I had left him. Only two factors were changed. No "shinny" was left — and lying open, with its miscellaneous contents strewed about, was the tin box. Rori somehow had managed to open it with the tiny key still clutched in his hand.

Concern for his safety alone was what made me notice the box. It was a receptacle for small fishing tackle of the sort carried here and there by any sportsman. Tangles of Dowagiac minnows, spoon hooks ranging in size to silver-backed number eights; three reels still carrying line of different weights, spinners, casting plugs, wobblers, floating baits, were spilled out upon the rough plank flooring where they might snag Rori badly if he rolled. I gathered them, intending to save him an accident.

With the miscellaneous assortment in my hands, however, I stopped dead. Something had caught my eye—something lying flush with the bottom of the lock box! I stared, and then swiftly tossed the hooks and other impedimenta upon the table. What I had glimpsed there in the box was a loose-leaf notebook of the sort used for recording laboratory data! And Rori scarcely could read let alone *write!*

Feverishly, a riot of recognition, surmise, hope and fear bubbling in my brain, I grabbed the book and threw it open. At once I knew that this was the end. The pages were scribbled in pencil, but the handwriting was that precise chirography I knew as belonging to John Corliss Cranmer, the scientist!

"... *Could he not have obeyed my instructions! Oh, God! This ...*"

These were the words at top of the first page which met my eye.

Because knowledge of the circumstances, the relation of which I pried out of the reluctant Rori only some days later when I had him in Mobile as a police witness for the sake of my friend's vindication, is necessary to understanding, I shall interpolate.

Rori had not told me everything. On his late visit to the vicinage of Dead House he saw more. A crouching figure, seated Turk fashion on top of the wall appeared to be writing industriously. Rori recognized the man as Cranmer, yet did not hail him. He had no opportunity.

Just as the Cajan came near, Cranmer rose, thrust the notebook, which had rested across his knees, into the box. Then he turned, tossed outside the wall both the locked box and a ribbon to which was attached the key.

Then his arms raised toward heavens. For five seconds he seemed to invoke the mercy of Power beyond all of man's scientific prying. And finally he leaped, *inside. . . .!*

Rori did not climb to investigate. He knew that directly below this portion of wall lay the mud sink into which he had thrown the chunks of meat!

VIII

This is a true transcription of the statement I inscribed, telling the sequence of actual events at Dead House. The original of the statement now lies in the archives of the detective department.

Cranmer's notebook, though written in a precise hand, yet betrayed the man's insanity by incoherence and frequent repetitions. My statement has been accepted now, both by alienists and by detectives who had entertained different theories in respect to the case. It quashes the noisome hints and suspicions regarding three of the finest Americans who ever lived — and also one queer supposition dealing with supposed criminal tendencies in poor Joe, the octoroon.

John Corliss Cranmer *went* insane for sufficient cause!

As readers of popular fiction know well, Lee Cranmer's *forte* was the writing of what is called — among fellows in the craft — the pseudo-scientific story. In plain words, this means a yarn, based upon solid fact in the field of astronomy, chemistry, anthropology or whatnot, which carries to logical conclusion improved theories of men who devote their lives to searching out further nadirs of fact.

In certain fashion these men are allies of science. Often they visualize something which has not been imagined even by the best of men from whom they secure data, thus opening new horizons of possibility. In a large way Jules Verne was one of these men in his day; Lee Cranmer bade fair to carry on the work in worthy fashion—work taken up for a period by an Englishman named Wells, but abandoned for stories of a different—and, in my humble opinion, less absorbing—type.

Lee wrote three novels, all published, which dealt with such subjects—two of the three secured from his own father's labors, and the other speculating upon the discovery and possible uses of inter-atomic energy. Upon John Corliss Cranmer's return from Prague that fatal winter, the father informed Lee that a greater subject than any with which the young man had dealt, now could be tapped.

Cranmer, senior, had devised a way in which the limiting factors in protozoic life and *growth*, could be nullified; in time, and with cooperation of biologists who specialized upon *karyokinesis* and embryology of higher forms, he hoped—to put the theory in pragmatic terms—to be able to grow swine the size of elephants, quail or woodcock with breasts from which a hundred-weight of white meat could be cut away, and steers whose dehorned heads might butt at the third story of a skyscraper!

Such result would revolutionize the methods of food

supply, of course. It also would hold out hope for all undersized specimens of humanity—provided only that if factors inhibiting growth could be deleted, some methods of stopping gianthood also could be developed.

Cranmer the elder, through use of an undescribed (in the notebook) growth medium of which one constituent was agar-agar, and the use of radium emanations, had succeeded in bringing about apparently unrestricted growth in the paramoecium protozoan, certain of the vegetable growths (among which were bacteria), and in the amorphous cell of protoplasm known as the amoeba—the last a single cell containing only neucleolus, neucleus, and a space known as the contractile vacuole which somehow aided in throwing off particles impossible to assimilate directly. This point may be remembered in respect to the piles of lumber left near the outside walls surrounding Dead House!

When Lee Cranmer and his wife came south to visit, John Corliss Cranmer showed his son an amoeba—normally an organism visible under low-power microscope—which he had absolved from natural growth inhibitions. This amoeba, a rubbery, amorphous mass of protoplasm, was of the size then of a large beef liver. It could have been held in two cupped hands, placed side by side.

"How large could it grow?" asked Lee, wide-eyed and interested.

"So far as I know," answered his father, "there is *no* limit—now! It might, if it got food enough, grow to be as big as the Masonic Temple!

"But take it out and kill it. Destroy the organism utterly—burning the fragments—else there is no telling what might happen. The amoeba, as I have explained, reproduces by simple division. Any fragment remaining might be dangerous."

Lee took the rubbery, translucent giant cell — but he did not obey orders. Instead of destroying it as his father had directed, Lee thought out a plan. Suppose he should grow this organism to tremendous size? Suppose, when the tale of his father's accomplishment were spread, an ameoba of many tons weight could be shown in evidence? Lee, of somewhat sensational cast of mind, determined instantly to keep secret the fact that he was not destroying the organism, but encouraging its further growth. Thought of possible peril never crossed his mind.

He arranged to have the thing fed — allowing for normal increase of size in an abnormal thing. It fooled him only in growing much more rapidly. When he came back from Cuba the amoeba practically filled the whole of the mud sink hollow. He had to give it much greater supplies. . . .

The giant cell came to absorb as much as two hogs in a single day. During daylight, while hunger still was appeased, it never emerged, however. That remained for the time that it could secure no more food near at hand to satisfy its ravenous and increasing appetite.

Only instinct for the sensational kept Lee from telling Peggy, his wife, all about the matter. Lee hoped to spring a *coup* which would immortalize his father, and surprise his wife terrifically. Therefore, he kept his own counsel — and made bargains with the Cajan, Rori, who supplied food daily for the shapeless monster of the pool.

The tragedy itself came suddenly and unexpectedly.

Peggy, feeding the two Gordon setters that Lee and she used for quail hunting, was in the Lodge yard before sunset. She romped alone, as Lee himself was dressing.

Of a sudden her screams cut the still air! Without her knowledge, ten-foot *pseudopods*—those flowing tentacles of protoplasm sent forth by the sinister occupant of the pool—slid out and around her putteed ankles.

For a moment she did not understand. Then, at first suspicion of the horrid truth, her cries rent the air. Lee, at that time struggling to lace a pair of high shoes, straightened, paled, and grabbed a revolver as he dashed out.

In another room a scientist, absorbed in his note-taking, glanced up, frowned, and then—recognizing the voice—shed his white gown and came out. He was too late to do aught but gasp with horror.

In the yard Peggy was half engulfed in a squamous, rubbery something which at first he could not analyze.

Lee, his boy, was fighting with the sticky folds, and slowly, surely, losing his own grip upon the earth!

IX

John Corliss Cranmer was by no means a coward, he stared, cried aloud, then ran indoors, seizing the first two weapons which came to hand—a shotgun and hunting knife which lay in sheath in a cartridged belt across hook of the hall-tree. The knife was ten inches in length and razor keen.

Cranmer rushed out again. He saw an indecent fluid something—which as yet he had not had time to classify—lumping itself into a six-foot-high center before his very eyes!

It looked like one of the micro-organisms he had studied! One grown to frightful dimensions. An amoeba!

There, some minutes suffocated in the rubbery folds —yet still apparent beneath the glistening ooze of this monster—were two bodies.

They were dead. He knew it. Nevertheless he attacked the flowing, senseless monster with his knife. Shot would do no good. And he found that even the deep, terrific slashes made by his knife closed together in a moment and healed. The monster was invulnerable to ordinary attack!

A pair of *pseudopods* sought out his ankles, attempting to bring him low. Both of these he severed—and escaped. Why did he try? He did not know. The two whom he had sought to rescue were dead, buried under folds of this horrid thing he knew to be his own discovery and fabrication.

Then it was that revulsion and insanity came upon him.

There ended the story of John Corliss Cranmer, save for one hastily scribbled paragraph—evidently written at the time Rori had seen him atop the wall.

May we not supply with assurance the intervening steps?

Cranmer was known to have purchased a whole pen of hogs a day or two following the tragedy. These animals never were seen again. During the time the wall was being constructed is it not reasonable to assume that he fed the giant organism within—to keep it quiet? His scientist brain must have visualized clearly the havoc and horror which could be wrought by the loathsome thing if it ever were driven by hunger to flow away from the Lodge and prey upon the countryside!

With the wall once in place, he evidently figured that starvation or some other means which he could supply would kill the thing. One of the means had been made by setting fire to several piles of the disgorged timbers; probably this had no effect whatever.

The amoeba was to accomplish still more destruction. In the throes of hunger it threw its gigantic, formless strength against the house walls *from the inside;* then every edible morsel within was assimilated, the logs, rafters and other fragments being worked out through the contractile *vacuole.*

During some of its last struggles, undoubtedly, the side wall of brick was weakened—not to collapse, however, until the giant amoeba no longer could take advantage of the breach.

In final death lassitude, the amoeba stretched itself out in a thin layer over the ground. There it succumbed, though there is no means of estimating how long a time intervened.

The last paragraph in Cranmer's notebook, scrawled so badly that it is possible some words I have not deciphered correctly, read as follows:

"In my work I have found the means of creating a monster. The unnatural thing, in turn, has destroyed my work and those whom I held dear. It is in vain that I assure myself of innocence of spirit. Mine is the crime of presumption. Now, as expiation —worthless though that may be—I give myself. . . ."

It is better not to think of that last leap, and the struggle of an insane man in the grip of the dying monster.

Late Night Final
By Stuart H. Stock

To survive in the city, you'd better learn the Rules.

Late Night Final

by Stuart H. Stock

David first became aware of . . . *them* . . . at the age of eleven. In New York, there exists a phenomenon known as the candy store. A candy store doesn't just sell candy. It may have a soda fountain, paperback books, toys, school supplies—a little of everything and not enough of anything. But every candy store sells magazines and newspapers.

When David was in grade school, living in Brooklyn, he used to walk past Schwartz's candy store on his way to P.S. 117 five days a week. The cramped little store cowered on a gray Brooklyn corner next to a hardware store, some three blocks from the nearest subway station.

The front window of the place was narrow and streaked with brownish filth so David could never look through it, and the sign hanging over the door said nothing more than "Drink Coca-Cola," with a picture in faded greens, reds, and browns of a hamburger partially devoured by the weather.

Schwartz's was still closed when David passed it each morning at about seven. But every morning he'd see great bundles of newspapers and magazines bound together with heavy, coarse string, left for the store by the distributor's truck while darkness pressed down upon the city.

David saw the bundles every day, rain or shine. The magazines and newspapers seemed there for the taking. The streets were still fairly empty at that time of morning, the subway rush for Manhattan not ready to begin for a good half hour. It would have been easy to slip a *New York Times* or a *Daily News* from the bundles—or ten or twenty for your friends. Or a copy of *Time* or the latest comic books—or even a *Playboy*.

Yet David noticed the bundles were never touched. In fact, the few people on the street at that hour seemed to studiously avoid even looking at them, walking past them as if they were invisible, going out of their way to avoid even coming close to them—as if the magazines and newspapers were infected with some withering disease and the merest touch might convey the pestilence to them.

David sensed a living fear on that street as people hurried by not looking at the papers or each other. Later, when he was older, David realized it was the same kind of fear he saw in the faces of people photographed on the streets of Berlin during the Nazis, or today in Moscow. And slowly he felt that same fear sliding its hands over him, till its decaying arms enveloped him completely.

David finally asked his mother to explain this peculiar thing he'd seen. She was a thin, haggard woman, with hollow cheeks and unlit eyes, but when he asked about the newspapers her face tightened and her eyes brightened as if with fever.

"Don't ask stupid questions, David," she said quickly. And that was all she'd say.

David went to his father—a small, intense man who made his living as an accountant—and repeated his question. His father put down his cigar and the newspaper he'd been reading, leaning close to David so the boy could smell the sour odor of the cigar on his breath.

"If you ever touch those papers," his father said, "something terrible will happen to you."

A chill raced through David's body. "What?" he asked.

"Never mind," his father answered, shaking his head. "Just remember."

Frustrated, David went so far as to ask Mr. Schwartz, the owner of the candy store. He was a fat man with a large, round face and a fringe of hair surrounding his shiny scalp.

His reaction to David's question was to roll his huge bulging eyes, looking around the little store as if, David thought, someone were listening to them.

"I don't got no time for crazy questions, kid," he said finally, and waddled away.

This only intensified David's curiosity, of course. Once, he even played hooky from school, getting up extra early to station himself across the street from Schwartz's in a doorway, watching from 6:30 in the morning when the papers were delivered, to 7:45 when Mr. Schwartz arrived to open the store.

David searched for some clue to tell him what protected those bundles. He stared hard into the frightened, worried faces of the people who went by, looking for some sign that might reveal the source of their fear.

By now David thought it was obvious that someone had to be watching those papers. But he never saw the police drive by, and Schwartz didn't live over the store or even nearby. So who, *who*, was protecting those papers, and why did it provoke such fear in his parents, in Mr. Schwartz, and in every person who walked the city streets?

When David was fourteen his family moved to another part of Brooklyn, leaving Schwartz's candy store behind. His father began sending David to buy his newspaper at a candy store near the elevated subway platform.

The place had no name so far as David knew. It lay in the middle of the block between a coffee shop and a drugstore. At night, with stores on either side brightly lit, the dim little candy store seemed to gape like a dark mouth on the street, swallowing the people who came rushing off the subway.

David noticed this new store had an innovation Schwartz's lacked. There was a window that could be opened to the street so you could take papers and magazines from an outside newsstand and pay without going inside the store.

But many times people buying papers didn't hand the man inside their change. He might be in the back of the store near the fountain or on the telephone. Instead, they simply left their money in a tray on the window counter.

A lot of change collected in that tray. Once David counted over ten dollars. Not that much—but enough to make stealing it worthwhile if you could do it without being seen.

But the money was never touched. Sometimes David watched from the darkness under the subway platform, waiting for someone to pocket the mound of change and bills, but no one ever did. Each person would pay or make change in a kind of ritualistic gesture—depositing the money, then moving the head back and forth once or twice before they faded away again into the night.

David occasionally thought about taking the money himself, it seemed so easy. But each time he began to reach for it the hairs would prickle on the back of his neck, and something like a cold, damp breath, tinged faintly with the smell of ammonia, would engulf him, making him shiver. Yet when he turned around there was never anybody behind him.

Sometimes, returning from dates or parties late at night, David heard noises behind him. Not footsteps—but something lighter and less palpable, like the chitterings of monkeys or the scurrying of rats' feet. His body would stiffen with fear and his steps become faster. But nothing ever bothered him.

Once, however, David managed to force his fear into the shape of resolution. He retraced his steps, ready if necessary to run. But all he found was a large wet spot on the sidewalk, revealed in the vague yellowish light of a streetlamp. The air reeked with an overpowering ammoniac odor that made his nostrils twitch. And in the bushes across the street he heard those same rustling, twittering noises like the gibbering of a lunatic.

And then there was the Madman. David was 17, getting ready to attend the City University in the fall. His parents were away for the weekend, leaving him alone in the house. He watched TV till midnight, and when he finally shut it off the house was instantly invaded by the low whisperings of a city night: the whine of cars speeding past, the hiss of wind in the trees and around the houses, the rise and fall of voices of late-night passers-by.

David checked the doors and windows and went to bed.

He was awakened by a finger holding in the front door bell; the ringing sounded like fingernails scraping through rust. David looked at the clock. It was a little past 3 A.M.

He got out of bed, starting for the door. And then came the voice:

"Oh my God," it wailed hoarsely, "Look at my face!" David froze. "Oh my God, Jesus Christ, look at my face. Please look at my face, oh please, oh please, oh please . . ."

David stood rigid, listening to the doorbell growling on and off and to the terrible twisted voice screaming for attention, his heart pounding in his chest.

He finally forced himself to go to the telephone and

dial 911 to call the police. A car would be over right away said the voice on the phone. In the meantime, it said, stay away from the doors and windows.

David went to the living room and sat trembling while the hideous voice screamed on and on, "Oh, God, Oh God, Dear God, just look at my face! Oh please, oh please. . ."

David sat there imagining what would happen if he opened the door—seeing a face bloody with shards of glass, or skin red and eaten by fire, or eyes blazing with madness. He shuddered and stayed where he was as the voice moaned on and on.

And then, in mid-sentence, it broke off. "What?" he heard it ask, a fragment of sanity seeming to return to it. "What are you doing? Keep away from me! What? What?"

There was a low gurgling cry—like someone being drawn under water—then nothing.

David didn't get up.

The police arrived a few minutes later and David went out on the porch with them. In the dull glow from the porchlight David noticed the porch was wet in spots, though it hadn't rained. And there was that vague ammonia-like odor in the cool night air, though the cops didn't seem to notice it. But nowhere was there evidence of his Madman.

It might have gone hard for David if the neighbors hadn't also heard the Madman's screams. The official explanation was that some drunk had picked the Sims' porch on which to vent his private demons, then wandered off. But there was nothing to show anything else had been there. The neighbors never heard his terrified reaction to whatever had come up on the porch after him.

David was convinced now that something else lived in the city besides people, something people didn't know about. They might suspect it, David thought; certainly they *sensed* the unseen presence. It showed in the narrow, constricted lives they led, bounded on all sides by fear, and in their worn, troubled faces.

The power which allowed that unseen presence to interfere in human lives frightened David beyond all measure. It terrified him that something could control an entire city through fear when it never even showed itself, never revealed its reasons or its motivations. How could you play the game if you didn't know *the rules?*

Of course, his experiences with this presence had so far been harmless, even benevolent. (Or had they? Perhaps his Madman had been their victim in more ways than one.)

But it was the sense of being controlled by them (somehow he *knew* there had to be more than one) that David feared and resented. And eventually he learned they could be malevolent when they wanted to.

It was his last summer during college. David was job-hunting in the lower end of Manhattan, near City Hall, but his efforts had been fruitless.

He entered the subway, finding himself on the East Side-Lexington Avenue line of the IRT; to get home he needed the West Side-7th Avenue line. David was still unsure of himself on the subways, but he thought his problem was solved when he spotted a sign with an arrow pointing: 7TH AVE. LINE THIS WAY.

David followed the sign down a flight of steps to a

tunnel—a murky gray passage littered with blackened gum and cigarette wrappers, the walls scrawled with obscenities in red paint, the whole place stinking of liquor and urine. But he went through it casually, like any New Yorker does—knowing this is the price of living where you live.

On the other side of the tunnel was another sign and then another. David followed the signs and arrows almost religiously: up and down stairs, across platforms, through more dark, filthy tunnels till he felt like a rat lost in a maze. It seemed to go on forever—yet he never passed another person. But when he came to the last sign and followed it out, he was shocked to find himself *back where he'd started*.

Getting lost once in the subway was nothing, yet David felt vaguely uneasy. He ignored the sensation and set out to follow the signs again, keeping watch for where he'd made his mistake. But when he left the final passage he was once more back where he'd begun.

A shiver rose towards his neck. He started out again, and as he walked the dirty, foul-smelling passages he heard a familiar noise behind him—a chittering like the muted humming of insects, and then the faint ammoniac smell rising above even the dead odors of cigarette smoke and beer and urine. The sounds grew louder in the dimness, the smell stronger, as if the source were closing in on him.

Sweat broke out on his forehead and he walked faster, trying to control the heaving of his chest as the sounds rose and fell behind him, coming closer then dropping back.

And when he broke into the light this time he was

on a different platform and a sign announced: WEST-SIDE 7TH AVE. LINE.

David drew a long deep breath, feeling it whistle hollowly in his chest. They'd been playing with him, he realized—deforming his reality to see what he'd do, the way a child will crush an anthill and watch the insects uncomprehending frenzy as they try to escape their unseen tormentor.

David felt himself grow angry; he didn't like being a plaything. There was a transit cop on the platform standing near a candy machine, and David walked over to him quickly.

"Listen," he began, "something was following me back there." He pointed back over his shoulder.

The cop inclined his head towards David. He was a tall man with a broad face, lined with fatigue. "Who was following you?" he asked.

"*Something* was following me," David repeated, and as he saw the frown grow across the cop's face, David caught the reflection of the white-faced, wild-eyed teenager in the cracked mirror of the candy machine behind the cop.

"Forget it," David said abruptly and walked away. From the corner of his eye he saw the cop go through the turnstile and saunter over to the change booth to regale the attendant with the story of one more nut spawned by the city.

David bit back his anger, feeling like a fool. The only other person nearby was an older woman carrying a shopping bag some twenty feet away. He shrugged to himself and leaned over the edge of the platform, looking down the tunnel. He saw the yellow spot of the train come out of the darkness and felt the vibrations under his feet. If the train was an express it wouldn't be stopping here. He leaned out a little further to try and make out the markings.

And then something pushed him.

David felt himself falling, felt his shoulder collide with metal, pain exploding in it—followed by a dozen other explosions throughout his body. He heard a scream and shouts and then the angry rumbling all around him.

With remarkable clarity David looked around and saw a shallow niche in the base of the platform. He threw himself into it, pressing himself back as tightly as he could, tasting bitter fright in his mouth.

The train roared past him deafeningly, the wind ripping at his clothes, tearing the breath from his lungs while a burning electrical smell stung his nostrils and he kept his eyes tightly shut.

The subway cars whipped by in seconds. David allowed himself to relax, his body falling forward. He realized dimly there was an electrified rail he should be trying to avoid.

Then someone was beside him helping him—the cop he realized—and other hands were pulling him back to the platform.

Yes, he was all right. No, he didn't need an ambulance. They were grouped around him—the cop, the attendant, the woman with the bag, and several others who'd appeared. The cop and the attendant were staring at him hard.

"I'm fine," David said breathlessly. "Just a little bruised. I guess I leaned out too far." But David knew that wasn't it. His attempt to inform the cop of *their* existence had been noticed, and in return he had received a warning.

David got a job after college as a copywriter for a small Manhattan advertising firm. He moved into a small, furnished apartment in a building in the east fifties that had been dressed over on the outside to make it look younger. It was only slightly beyond his means.

David tried hard to ignore his secret enemies, and they left him mostly alone. But several times on his way home from work in the evening, David boarded subway trains marked clearly for uptown; then, after several stops, he'd realize suddenly he was heading *down*town. A helpless, burning anger would grow inside him then, but there was nothing he could do. He sensed it was *their* way of telling him he had not been forgotten.

Late at night, if he brought work home from the office, and the city was nearly silent, David heard the rat/insect/monkey noises outside his door. Some of it was the building settling, he supposed. But he knew *they* were also out there, prowling in the darkened hallways.

David realized he wasn't being singled out. From what he saw around him they played with everyone, dominated the life of every person in the city according to their vicious whims. How else to explain the mysteries of city life?

Why was it that when you waited for a taxi, half a dozen buses would speed mockingly by—and when you wanted the bus, the streets overflowed with taxis?

Why was it when you came to a corner where the traffic light was green, it took only five steps off the curb until it turned red, leaving you to fight for your life in the face of oncoming traffic?

And why was it that when you satisfied yourself the street was clear and began to cross that a truck would magically appear and come within inches of running you down? And who, or what, reached out to jerk you out of its way when no one else was anywhere near you?

Of course sometimes the person *wasn't* pulled out of the way; sometimes the person didn't escape from the speeding traffic in time. Dozens of people were struck by cars and trucks in the city every day. People fell on the subway tracks or out of windows or from roofs all the time. Some of those were accidents, but some, David knew, were not.

And what of the thousands of people who came to the city each year and then simply disappeared without a trace?

How was it, David wondered, that New Yorkers could ignore the most outrageous things happening around them; bodies lying in the gutter, screams for help, crimes committed before their eyes? What was it that made people walk the streets, their shoulders hunched, their eyes averted, terror caught in every motion, every step?

How could all this happen?—unless something made it happen; something that could distort reality to ensure the people of the city followed its insane rules and lived their lives at the mercy of its whims and pleasures. And it left those people to exist in a murky gray world without dignity, self-respect, or human feeling.

Yet no one but David seemed to be aware of these

things. At parties or office bull sessions people talked about coincidences: of invisible hands nearly pushing them onto the subway tracks; or stores open one day and gone the next; of getting lost in parts of the city they knew perfectly well.

They appeared unwilling to acknowledge the absurdity of such occurrences—to make the rational leap David had made. Instead, they'd sip their scotches or their coffees and talk about luck or absent-mindedness. Yet there was always that furtive look around, the nervous darting of the eyes that said, *I sense there is something peculiar in all this, but it would probably be better not to know what it is.*

And then David fell in love.

There had been other women in his life over the years, but this was something new for David. Sheila was a new employee in the graphics department of the agency where David worked—though she'd lived in New York all her life—and their work threw them together. She had red hair and the kind of large, dazzling green eyes only redheads are allowed to have. Slowly, a warm bond grew between them as they shared their common backgrounds, their lives.

One night, at dinner in a small Italian restaurant with checkered tablecloths and candles in wine bottles, Sheila described to David how that afternoon something had pushed her into the path of a speeding bus, yanking her back at the last second. Yet she'd been entirely alone at the time.

David felt his face grow hot with rage, his fists clenching so hard his nails dug into his palms, the blood pounding in his temples. Attacking him was one thing, but this attack on someone he loved was the ultimate provocation.

Before he knew it, he was pouring out all his experiences and suspicions about the strange powers that ruled the city. When he'd finished, Sheila sat staring at him, her eyes wide with sudden terror.

"It sounds crazy, I know," David said, feeling their relationship teeter on the edge of oblivion.

Sheila cleared her throat. "It's an interesting idea," she said.

David knew then that he had lost her.

For the rest of the evening she was friendly but distant, and in the days that followed she went out of her way to avoid him at the office. Slowly, the warmth that had been so strong between them turned into bitter cold.

David's anger approached madness. *They* had done this to him. They had played with him, manipulated him, tormented him all his life. And now they had stolen from him the one thing he cared most about in his life.

He had to do something. Once and for all, he would expose them, force them out into the open. And once everyone in the city knew about them, their power would come to an end.

Slowly, a plan took shape in his mind.

It went back to the very first hint he'd had of their existence—the bundled newspapers on the street. An attempt to steal them would surely bring the mysterious "guardians" out of hiding.

First, David bought an infra-red movie camera. He spent two weeks learning how to use it properly. Then he began haunting one of the neighborhood bars—a dark hole of a place called *Tony's*.

He eavesdropped on the conversations of the regular customers, finally picking on one who looked a little shabbier than the others, a little more in need, but who made it clear he didn't care how his needs were met.

David sat down at the bar next to him and struck up a conversation. His name was Jensen. He was an older man—well over forty, David guessed—a man whose face was guarded and withdrawn, the eyes always moving, looking desperately for something he'd never found in the city.

After several drinks, he offered Jensen $100 to steal the newspapers while David filmed him in the act.

Jensen stiffened. "You from the cops?" he asked.

"No. Let's just say I made a bet that it could be done."

The other man said nothing. David took out his wallet and laid two fifty dollar bills on the table. "You can have that now," he said. "And another fifty when the job's finished."

Jensen's mouth worked for a second—then his hand snaked out for the bills. "Okay, mister," he said. "You got a deal."

David had already picked a candy store on a corner a few blocks away; it reminded him of Schwartz's. It was chilly when they got there, around two in the morning. The darkness was overcast with clouds that hid the moon and would make the dawn come late. The only light came from the feeble streetlamp in the middle of the block and the few stray snatches from the electric signs and window lights left on by shop-keepers in a vain attempt to discourage burglars.

They took up a position in a doorway across the street. Jensen tried several times to start a conversation, but David answered only in monosyllables, and eventually the other man gave up.

At almost six-thirty the grim, early-morning silence was broken by the rumbling of a truck. It stopped at the corner and an already tired-looking teenager in a leather jacket pushed several large bundles off the back of the truck to the sidewalk.

David waited until the truck was gone, then nodded to Jensen. He lifted the camera and began to film.

Jensen walked confidently across the street. He looked around, saw no one on the wet, gray street. He bent down, hoisted a wire-bound bundle of news-papers marked "Late Night Final" and began to cross the street again.

He didn't get five steps, though . . .

David's breath froze in his lungs. In the near-darkness he suddenly saw shapes emerge—from where he wasn't sure.

They were fat, doughy things of varying shades of gray—some almost a sickly white, while others were so black they stood out sharply in the dimness. They varied in size from slightly taller than a man to that of a small child. And there seemed to be dozens of them.

They plunged through the air at Jensen, as if being sucked towards some great vacuum. Jensen threw the newspapers aside, giving one short cry before they enveloped him.

David could only see his head now, the rest of him surrounded by the shapes, their flesh glistening and undulating like a worm's. They were squeezing Jensen between them. The stench of ammonia was everywhere.

There was a muffled crack from the mass on the street, and Jensen's head seemed to collapse and disappear into it. A translucent pinkish jelly began to ooze from between the great shapes to the street.

David's stomach heaved. His throat was tight and his heart pounded wildly. It was an effort to keep filming.

The shapes separated now, revealing nothing left between them but the pinkish slime on the street. One of the smaller ones brushed against the bundle, shoving it back towards the curb. They started to disperse, ready to mix again invisibly with the night and the city.

The smell of ammonia was overpowering and David felt suddenly dizzy. He reeled back, lowering the camera—and it slid from his sweaty grip, falling to the ground with a clatter.

One of the shapes turned.

David wasn't sure it *saw* him—he couldn't make out anything like eyes—but it knew he was there. And then those great, wet shapes began to cross the street.

The image of Jensen being crushed to pulp flared in David's brain, the speed with which the creatures had swept through the air to engulf him in their pale, moist flesh.

There was no time to pick up the camera. David bolted from the doorway and ran, never looking back, hardly seeing anything in the darkened city. His lungs were bursting and his legs felt brittle, but each time he slowed his pace he was sure he could hear an insane twittering begin to rise around him, and he forced himself to go on.

How long he ran he didn't know. His legs grew numb and his sides ached. A gray mist seemed to have descended, so the objects around him appeared hazy, indistinct. Finally, he staggered to a stop, lurching against a building, clinging to its side for support.

He looked around, chest still heaving, sweat running into his eyes. He shook his head to try and clear it.

Nothing looked familiar. He had no idea where he was, and in the gray fog he could see no street signs. There were only the buildings around him, towering off into the grayness where they disappeared. Before him lay the wide avenue, stretching off in both directions until it too was lost in the mist.

His panting slowed, and dull pain began to return to his numbed legs—and with that pain came the realization of what he'd done.

He was responsible for what had happened to Jensen. He had sent the man into the street, knowing what would happen to him. It didn't matter who Jensen was, where he came from, or what he did—he was a human being—and he had sent the man to his death without a second thought.

A vision of Jensen's body disappearing between those bloated forms overcame him, and a wave of nausea swept through his body, followed by great, wracking sobs that left him cringing against the wall of the building.

Something in the streets sang to him then. A low, hoarse melody flowed from the mists around him. David straightened as he inclined his head, searching for the source of the voice from the grayness.

He took a step forward, and the whispering tones seemed to invade his mind, blotting out the thoughts and emotions of a moment ago. He couldn't remember them, couldn't *feel* them.

Dimly, he felt his flesh begin to melt and flow. He felt his limbs grow thick and heavy, his body reshaping itself. His brain was numb. In his mind there was only . . . grayness, a blank and empty malevolence that hungered for satisfaction.

In the grayish dawn, the great pallid shape, its wet skin glistening, lumbered off in search of its companions in the city—a city full of things.

The Vengeance of Yig
By Lin Carter

A new tale in the "Cthulhu Mythos"—

The Vengeance of Yig

by Lin Carter

So repulsive was the degree of decadence into which the languid inhabitants of K'n-yan had declined in recent cycles, that I found myself increasingly alienated from my own kind. The tedium of their immortality and the lassitude of their lives had led them to bizarre and bestial pleasures, into endless erotic experimentations, and into a feverish questing after new and novel sensations which became ever more repugnant to me.

Surely it could not be that I, Z'hu-Gthaa, savant of the Ninth Circle, had become the only intellect in Tsath who retained his studious and scientific dedication. Such, however, seemed to be the situation, and at length I resolved to quit forever the ancient city and eloign to some remote bourn where I might continue my work in the uninterrupted solitude I required.

My first step in this plan involved my taking up residence in L'thaa, an abandoned suburb of Tsath. While a work-party of the *gyaa-yothn*, the artificial man/beast hybrids we of the cavern-world employed as beasts of burden, transported my notes and folios, my instruments and equipment, to a once-splendid manse now lapsed sadly into decay but still eminently servicable, I pondered my future movements. The program of studies upon which I had embarked were devoted to the antique lore found in the Yothic manuscripts, those half-decipherable records left behind aeons earlier by the former residents of red-litten Yoth, the cavern-world beneath our own. They had been a race of reptilian quadrupeds who had sought refuge in Yoth upon the demolition of their primordial continent, long ago reft asunder by geological forces and drowned beneath the steaming seas of the Elder World. Accounting themselves the spawn of Yig, Father of Serpents, they had served that divinity as his minions under the leadership of undying Sss'haa, who of old menaced mankind in age-forgotten Valusia.

At some point in their interminable history (which by aeons antedates the evolution of men), the dwellers in Yoth unaccountably rejected the worship of Yig in favor of black, amorphous Tsathoggua. Whereupon the race sank into desuetude in a mysterious manner, and from some cryptic cause; eventually abandoning Yoth, the remnants of the Serpent-people fled to regions adjacent to the boreal Pole and took residence in the noisome caverns subterraneous to Mount Voormithadreth. The reasons for their flight, as for their decay, yet remain an enigma, albeit one which I had long ago determined to solve.

In epochs prior to mine own, when the inhabitants of

K'n-yan had been a hardier, more adventurous breed, certain explorers had dared the unknown perils of redly-litten Yoth, returning with those manuscripts to which I have above alluded. For untold cycles the Yothic scrolls were pondered by savants, a study resultant in a vast rebirth of philosophic and scientific advancement, for the Serpent-folk were adepts far superior to the best our kind could produce, and their arcana was at once baffling, abstruse and recondite.

In their enthusiasm for the Yothic lore, the people of K'n-yan unwisely adopted the worship of Tsathoggua, purloining his curious eidola from their onyx pedestals in the black basaltic temples erected by the Serpent-folk. While, prior to their adoption of the alien divinity, they had celebrated the mysteries of Shub-Niggurath the Mighty Mother and her awesome Sons, Nug, Yeb and Yig himself, our ancestors entertained no trepidations at this heretical desertion of the Old Gods, as their hierophants deemed Tsathoggua none other than the veritable sire of the aforesaid Nug, Yeb and Yig, having mated with the Mighty Mother at some remote period before his own descent to this planet.

It was my ambition to penetrate the innermost arcana of the Serpent-people, and to conquer the deepest secrets of their magistry.

During the lustrum I spent resident in the crumbling manse on the outskirts of Tsath, I delved ever deeper into the Yothic lore, at length exhausting those manuscripts fetched hither by the early explorers. That this was frustrating in the extreme the reader can readily imagine, for I had by no means approached the terminus of my studies. There was no other course to follow, but that I must descend into that tenebrous and carmine-litten netherworld beneath our own, in hope of salvaging further documents.

The site of the portal by which to gain access to Yoth was a secret lost in the obscurity of ages, but antique legends whispered that it was situated somewhere amidst the plains of Nith, perhaps in the valley of Hoy-Dha. Together with a work-party of those of the *gyaa-yothn* assigned to me, and guarded by the vigilance of nine *y'm-bhi* (the animated cadavers we of K'n-yan used as slave-labor), I removed to the plains of Nith and sought the vale which lay cupped in the Grh-yan hills beyond the ruined city of Quum.

Deserted of men, the vale of Hoy-Dha was desolate and inhospitable, and was rumored the haunt of certain flesh-eating predatory lizards called the *yukkoth*. Shielded by the vigilance of my nine resuscitated cadavers, however, I had little to fear even from the monstrous and shambling *yukkoth,* for it is exceptionally difficult to slay anything that is already, and long since, quite dead. We began our work at once, for neither my hybrids nor my zombie-like slaves required rest or sustenance, any more than did I, and the misty upper reaches of this cavern-world are eternally permeated by an azure luminance that wavers not, neither does it ever fail.

Within the desolation of Hoy-Dha I at length perceived a monolithic slab of stone so situated as if to conceal the mouth of a pit. It was no task at all to the tireless vigor of my servitors to pry away this stone (marked, I could not help but notice, with a peculiar hieroglyphic sign or symbol in no language with which I was then familiar), which act accomplished, the entrance I had suspected was soon revealed. My *gyaa-yothn* descended therein by means of a gravitational device I had perfected, returning to report the passage blocked by innumerable tons of solid stone.

The removal of this haply afforded me no problem, for among the instruments I had carried hither was a mechanism which harnessed the magnetic field of the planet, focussed into an all-penetrating beam which dissolved the bonds of molecular attraction which alone hold the particles of matter together. Erelong the way was cleared for my descent into the netherworld.

I found myself on a bleak plain whose expanse was encumbered by the wreckage of an immense city which I at once recognized from the descriptions of it found within the Yothic manuscripts as none other than primordial Zzoon, which in former cycles had served as residence to the priesthood of the ophidian race. But, in this illimitable litter of ruin, where might I find that which I sought?

By a broad avenue lined with monoliths of black obsidian, my slaves and I traversed the outer suburbs, approaching the heart of the vast necropolis. The scene was foreboding and I could not but dislike the brooding silence, the horror of that interminable decay of tumbled masonry, as it sprawled under the sanguinary glare of the dim and crimson radiance which pervades the vastness of Yoth. My perturbations were in no wise decreased when at length I perceived that we were not entirely alone in this titanic landscape of shattered stone; for innumerous serpents slithered about the colossal wreckage, their unhealthily-mottled and abnormally-grown coils of an appalling size.

Passing beneath a crumbling arch of basalt, I was alarmed when one of the enormous serpents dropped upon the anthropoidal shoulders of the foremost of my *gyaa-yothn* servitors. Despite its untiring vigor and the possession of a strength far transcending that of my own degenerate kind, the slave was crushed to a pulp in the inexorable coils. In my agitation, I disintegrated the head of the serpent with a beam from my atomic weapon; it vanished in a sizzling flare of actinic light, but it did naught to reassure me that the headless length squirmed away, vanishing into the ruins at a leisurely pace.

"It would seem that not all of the serpent-kind have quitted Yoth," I said with an attempt at bravado I would have found contemptible under circumstances other than these. "Let us proceed!"

At the center of that vast, wreckage-strewn plain we found a domed citadel of dark, nitre-eaten stone, in less disrepair than its neighboring edifices, wherein we took refuge from the monstrous serpents. My servitors ransacked the structure while I erected force-barriers against any unwonted entrance by the scaly denizens of the city. They returned at length lacking two of their number: another of the *gyaa-yothn* and one of the *y'm-bhi*, both presumably mangled or devoured by the prodigious ophidians.

During the time which followed, we explored the interminable chambers, corridors and crypts of the colossal structure, and at length a series of inscriptions were disclosed. I had become through my studies highly proficient in deciphering the minute cuneiform characters employed by the Serpent-people, but these were in a variant with which I was unfamiliar. They required an extensive perusal before I was able to un-riddle their meaning. When I did, I exclaimed with delight, for the inscriptions were no other than an account of the last days of Yoth, and a description of the events which led up to the abandonment of the cavern-world.

Misfortunately, the inexorable passage of time had flaked and gnawed the sleek basaltic surface of the wall, obliterating many key passages and entire columns of charactery. However, I made out enough of the inscription to deduce that it made frequent reference to a place or structure whose name I easily transliterated into the vocables of my own kind as "Ngoth." This Ngoth would seem intimately associated with the former cultus of Yig, later interdicted by the ophidian hierophants when that worship was superceded by the celebrants of Tsathoggua. From the frequency with which the name Ngoth recurred in the inscriptions, I could hazard an estimate of its premier importance in the decline of the Serpent-folk.

The inscriptions, however, provided no clue as to the whereabouts of this Ngoth; in time, however, the labors of my unwearying servitors excavated a vast pave in a rotunda of surprising extent. The pave had been littered by wreckage from the collapsing dome which had aforetime served as roof to the enormous chamber; when cleared of rubble it revealed itself sculptured with nothing less valuable than a relief-map of the entire expanse of the netherworld, upon which the sites of major centers and metropolises were marked with symbols of obvious meaning. Hence the location of Ngoth was rapidly discovered, and my party and I departed from Zzoon with precipitous haste, bound for the enigmatic Ngoth.

Although it lay a considerable distance from the ruined metropolis of the Serpent-people, we found, once we had left the outskirts of Zzoon, the way unimperilled by the prodigious serpents which had, by that point, reduced the number of my slaves to one-half. Dreary and desolate under the red glare was that expanse of plain, which the cartographic pavement termed "the Desolation of Thoon," but we pressed on without pause. I had begun to find the bleak and brooding silence of this somber waste, drenched in its bloody light, oppressive and almost frightful. Now did I begin to regret having ever dared descend into ill-rumored Yoth, and to curse the fervor of the savant that had goaded me to this extremity.

At length we arrived at Ngoth, discovering a grim and gloomy prospect. Before us yawned the mouth of an enormous, circular pit ringed about with megaliths of mottled, greenish-ochre stone. It was the circle of monoliths that I examined first, finding them minutely graven in the cuneiform of the Serpent-folk. Bathed in the bloody glare, the characters were unusually legible.

Upon those standing-stones I read a terrible chronicle of eldritch doom. I learned that the Serpent-people had, aeons ago, broken through the Earth's crust to discover a cavern-world under their own world of Yoth, and that it was even blackly-litten N'kai, the dominion of Tsathoggua, that Abomination which seeped down from the stars before the Earth was completely formed. Prodigious was the power commanded by Tsathoggua, bottomless the reservoirs of his wisdom, and the Serpent-folk were stricken with awe and amazement before him. They fell into idolatry, in their folly abandoning even the cultus of their awful Sire, Yig, Lord of Serpents; wherefore did Yig curse them with a mighty curse.

His vengeance did not at once take its toll, for wily and cunning is Yig, and, like all his scaly brood, somnolent and patient. But gradually a hideous change fell over the dwellers of Yoth, so that they lessened by gradations so minute that it was many cycles before even they perceived what had eventuated. Their hissing speech became labored, its natural sibilance thickened, slurring the language, until at length language itself fell into desuetude. The knowledge of writing became lost, the arts and sciences fell into a profound decay, and generation by generation, the Serpent-folk declined in intelligence as in stature.

Towards the end of their inexorable *devolution,* their quadrupedal limbs atrophied, dwindling away to nothing. At the end of it, the Serpentmen of Valusia, whose accomplishments were among the most prodigious of the mighty wonders of the Elder World, degenerated into mere squirming serpents, mindlessly wallowing in the foetor of their dark lairs amidst the crumbling wreckage of their immemorial civilization, mating loathsomely, feeding repellently upon their own offspring, in lieu of other sustenance.

When their gradual devolution was completed, then was the vengeance of Yig realized in all its horror: but by then it was too late. And in those last days, before the degeneration of the race had reached its ultimate nadir, the Serpent-priests implored aid of Tsathoggua, but gained not the guerdon of their worship.

In the end, naught but mindless serpents slithering through the ruined and abandoned temples of the

Black God were left, and the collapse of Yothic civilization was a doom such as no other empire in all the annals of intelligence hath ever known . . .

He who had recorded these fearful chronicles of the doom of Yoth was none other than Sss'haa, supreme hierophant of Yig. He and a small remnant of the Yothic kind, who had steadfastly cleaved to the Father of Serpents, were spared the horrible decline into squirming beasthood. Ere they fled in terror from accursed and fallen Yoth, they had with infinite toil set down that ghastly chronicle in perdurable and adamantine stone, for any that might come after to read of the vengeance of Yig.

And then I knew the place to which I had so rashly come . . .

I turned to stare into the mouth of that black pit, the Pit of Ngoth, and knew it for what it was, the Lair of Yig, into which the Elder Gods had hurled and imprisoned him under the spell of that arch-potent talisman, the Elder Sign!

The dank breath that panted up the dark throat of the Pit was cold with a transmundane frigor, and thick with the unholy reek of centuried and pustulent ophidian slime . . . what vast, sluggish, abominable Thing lay coiled and somnolent in the foetid depths, my numbed brain scarce dared conjecture . . . but I knew, with a grisly foreboding, that the denizens of Yoth, degenerate and mindless reptiles though they had long since become, would not for long permit our intrusion into that most sacred of all their shrines. And even as I turned to gaze out across the illimitable expanse of the Desolation of Thoon I knew what my eyes should behold. And, lo! it was even so, for the barren plain was buried beneath an undulant and teeming river of serpents . . . serpents of abnormal size, with the glint of a preternatural intelligence yet smouldering behind the mindless ferocity of their serpent-gaze . . .

The last of my slaves has gone down under the massive, slimy coils and I am now alone. Hundreds have I slain with my disintegrating beams, yet there are thousands more. They slither around and around the ring of standing-stones, and the sibilance of their hissing cries stabs into my brain, obscuring thought and freezing my very blood.

The atomic weapon is, alas, not inexhaustible, however potent its energies. The compressed radium which is the source of its power will erelong be consumed. When that moment comes . . .

This record I have set down, graven in a cylinder of imperishable metal, at intervals snatched from the labor of my defence; some enduring testament of my discovery must survive me, so that the inhabitants of blue-litten K'n-yan may know that Z'hu-Gthaa, savant of the Ninth Circle, hath transcended the accomplishments of all others, to penetrate the innermost secrets of the former denizens of Yoth.

The actinic glare sputters fitfully, and dies. The power-element is now exhausted.

The monstrous serpents pour like an obscene river, slithering between the standing-stones.

I would that my end could be other than it shall be. But I, too, shall feel the vengeance of Yig.

(continued from page 1)

forty-seven issues of the magazine. He appears in this issue with a new story, aptly entitled "Homecoming."

Our second "anniversary item" is the work of one of our most distinguished alumni, Mr. Ray Bradbury. While Mr. Long was the first major discovery of *WT's* most famous editor, Farnsworth Wright, Mr. Bradbury was an early discovery of Dorothy McIlwraith, who succeeded Farnsworth Wright to the prestigious editorial chair. His first story appeared in our issue for November, 1942, eighteen years after the debut of Frank Belknap Long, and over the years his distinctive short-stories have adorned some twenty-seven issues of *Wierd Tales*. His last appearance here was in our Fall, 1973 issue, while Mr. Long's last appearance here was in the issue dated Summer, 1974.

Between the two of these gifted gentlemen, then, they span most of the entire history of *Weird Tales* — two hundred and seventy-three issues, anyway — which explains why, to us, they represent the history of the Unique Magazine. And we are delighted to welcome them back to this sixtieth anniversary issue of the magazine in which they both were first published.

In each and every issue of this new series, it is our earnest endeavor to combine the newer authors with the old, if only to demonstrate the continuity of macabre literature to which *Weird Tales* has contributed so richly. We feel proud to be able to include in this special issue, then, what is believed to be the last story ever written by the late Robert Aickman, "The Next Glade."

Mr. Aickman is one of those authors of the macabre who rose to prominence too late to have submitted his excellent yarns to the Unique Magazine before it suspened regular publication in 1954. But, while he is unfortunately a stranger to these pages, he is certainly no stranger to the genre it represents, for he happens to be the grandson of the Edwardian novelist, Richard Marsh (whose super-thriller, *The Beetle,* was much admired by H.P. Lovecraft). It is fitting that Mr. Aickman makes his first appearance in this magazine in the same issue that also features a newly-discovered poem by Robert E. Howard, one of *Weird Tales'* most famous authors, making his one hundred and eleventh appearance here.

Our attempted balance between the newer authors and the old is also exemplified by the fact that a new story, "Calling Card," appears in this issue. It is the work of the superb young British writer, Ramsey Campbell, who, like Mr. Aickman, began writing professionally a little too late to have sold to the original *Weird Tales.* As well, let us call to your attention a fine novelette, "The City of Dread," by Lloyd Arthur Eshbach. For many years the publisher of Fantasy Press, Mr. Eshbach rarely had the time to craft his strong fictions for the pulp magazines, but it was our pleasure to have published his first story, "Isle of the Dead," in our October, 1936 issue. It is good to have him back with us again.

As usual, though, each of the four issues in this new revival of the oldest pulp magazine still being published must stress the discovery of new talent, for that writers, for they represent the future. So, with this issue, we welcome to these pages the diverse

talents of Charles Sheffield, James Anderson, and Stuart H. Stock, each making his first appearance in *Weird Tales*.

As well, two of our "regulars" reappear herein with brilliant new stories: John Brizzolara (who first appeared in our last issue), and Steve Rasnic Tem with a nightmarish little yarn, "Save the Children!." Actually, we can only claim the honor of having discovered Mr. Brizzolara, for Mr. Tem had some three stories published elsewhere, before coming home to *Weird Tales*. But, nonetheless, we regard both as *Weird Tales* regulars, and hope to continue featuring new tales from both of these excellent new writers.

One final word on this sixtieth anniversary issue, and then we will turn the page over to our correspondents. Our *Weird Tales* 'First' department has become a regular fixture in this new series, and for this very special issue it seems only fitting and proper to reprint a story from the very first issue of this magazine, that of March, 1923.

Among the twenty-four stories, and the first part of a serial, which appeared in that historic first issue, only one tale has survived the generations to become something of a modern classic in horror fiction. Often anthologized, it seems appropriate to reprint it at this time . . . "Ooze," by Anthony M. Rud.